BOOK FIVE OF THE DECEPTION SERIES
SEQUEL TO WILL OF DECEPTION

WOES

OF

DECEPTION

RYAN HODGE

SMP
PUBLISHING

SMP Publishing Edition

Printed in the United States of America

10 9 8 7 6 5 4 3 2 1

ISBN: 978-0-9977990-2-6 (PBK)

DEDICATION

Dear Ma,

We'll always appreciate the love that you showered us
with,
The love you blessed us with almost seems unreal-
something like a myth.
I cherish boyhood memories holding your leg while
walking down the Ave.,
All of the lessons of doing things the right way and all
the things I can have.
You taught us how to be independent and strong,
You always promoted to never skip steps even if the
process was long.
I remember every holiday we were five people deep,
Up playing cards and board games until we all fell
asleep.
These are things we cherish and the times we'll always
miss,
Because the love you poured on us was like being
bathed in bliss.
We love you always and forever,
At the forefront of our minds, we'll forget you never.

CHAPTER 1
Sage's Perspective

The doctor picks his head up from the floor, but is still avoiding eye contact. They say if the doctor doesn't look you in the eyes that the news is not good. Now, he's alternating between rubbing his face and his scalp.

"Come on doc, give it to me straight," I order.

The doctor lifts his head and slowly speaks, "Ms. Mills has lost a tremendous amount of blood and has sustained a lot of tissue damage. The bullets that hit her were hollow points and they're known for causing severe damage. She is alive, but is very weak. I don't know if she'll survive or not. She's in critical condition and the next forty-eight hours are crucial to her survival. She's lucky that the bullets didn't strike her directly because she'd be deceased for sure. She's also at a high risk for infection because the bullets traveled through another person before entering her."

I'm mad as hell right now. I could hurt myself for what I've done. If Sheena ends up dying, I'll never be able to forgive myself. I'll be the reason that my boys grow up without their mother. Everyone deserves to have their mother in their lives. Lord knows I don't know what I would have done without my mother growing up.

If Sheena dies, I wonder if the boys would blame me? Would they hate me and disown me as their father? I would surely have to tell them exactly what happened to Sheena. I'd hate to lose them, but I'd have to be honest with them. Even if I didn't tell them, they would eventually find out about it and potentially hate me even more for keeping it from them.

Rachel, Ilesha, and I all embrace after the doctor gives his report. They can't stop crying. To my surprise, Ilesha is more out of control with the sobbing than Rachel is.

"Can we see her doctor?" I ask.

"My best recommendation at this time is for her to be alone. She's in an extremely precarious state, so she needs all the rest she can get to try to overcome this injury. I'll send notice through the nurses when I feel she can be visited," says Dr. Cooper.

The doctor walks away leaving us to ponder whether we'll stay at the hospital or not. The boys hear the ladies crying and become agitated as well. I break our embrace and tend to my sons. After a minute of consoling them, they calm down and stop crying.

Rachel and Ilesha pick up Deric and Devin respectively. It's just the three of us right now. This is possibly how the boys will be raised if Sheena doesn't pull through.

"Ladies, thank you so much for being here. Also, I apologize for all of this. This entire fiasco is my fault," I utter.

Rachel replies, "You don't have to thank us for being here. Sheena is our sister and these are our godsons. It's our duty to be here and our responsibility. Don't blame yourself for the actions of Kevin and Eric. It's not your fault."

"This isn't your fault. If you hadn't done what you did, they would have killed all of us with the poison in the alcohol. You saved our lives, so stop with all the blame taking. We ride for Sheena and these precious princes, so you never have to thank us for being here and helping," Ilesha remarks.

"I understand, but I still feel complicit in all of this. I've played twenty different scenarios in my head of what I could have done differently, but I never find an answer. I should have told Sheena from the start that I was the boys' father and we'd all be somewhere totally different," I say.

"My brother, I understand how you feel, but we have to deal in what is because we can't deal in what is not or what should have been.

Blaming yourself changes nothing. My sister will still be in that room fighting for her life no matter who you blame," Rachel narrates.

"You're right," I say.

"Hell yeah she's right. These boys need you now more than ever, so all of that feeling sorry for yourself, Sheena, and the boys is not an option. Fuck shoulda, coulda, woulda cause that's not reality," Ilesha shoots in.

"I got it. You know I got my boys. Well, enough of the hypothetical talk then. Let's deal in the moment's issue," I speak.

Rachel rubs my back as she says, "We're here to help with whatever Sheena and the boys need. Don't hesitate to call."

I say, "Thanks, I won't."

"Well, I don't think the boys really need to be in this hospital all night, so I'm gonna take them home with me," says Ilesha.

"That's an excellent idea. These germs are not something they need to be exposed to at all and especially not overnight," I voice.

Rachel and Ilesha tell me that they're leaving and to contact them if anything changes. They pack the boys and their belongings up and exit the hospital. I know I have a long few nights ahead of me because I'm going to sleep here until Sheena recovers and goes home. I may need a new back after this is all over, but Sheena is the love of my life and I'm not leaving her side. I walk to the family room of the hospital. I fix myself a cup of tea and watch television while I sip the tea. About an hour later, I feel myself drifting, so I get a blanket and pillow from a nurse. I head back to the family room and get comfortable on the couch. Within minutes of sprawling on the couch, I am asleep.

CHAPTER 2
Sage's Perspective

The next morning, I'm violently awakened by a sharp pain that shoots up my back like a comet shooting through outer space. I'm not surprised that I'm experiencing pain from my terrible sleeping accommodations, but I didn't expect the pain to arrive so soon. It's normally a few days before I endure back pain from sleeping on a couch. Even when I do have back pain, the pain is never this severe.

What time is it? I look over at the clock and see that it's roughly one o'clock in the afternoon. I don't know what time I eventually fell asleep, but I definitely didn't want to sleep this late. I hope Sheena is doing better today. Hopefully, she's awake and I'll be able to see her. I need to wash my face and brush my teeth at a bare minimum before I go find somebody to get some answers from. I get up and head to the bathroom and freshen up a little bit. When I come out of the bathroom, I stop by the nurse's station.

"Hi, my name is Sage McMillian and I'm Ms. Mills' fiancé. She's the one who suffered the gunshot wounds. I was hoping to talk to a doctor to get an update on how she's doing and I'm hoping to see her. The doctor from last night said that he'd be around today," I say.

The lady at the nurse station responds, "Ms. Mills is doing okay. She's still pretty weak, but the doctor expects her to pull through. She won't be up and running for a while, but she's in a much better position from last night. The doctor saw you sleeping in the lounge and didn't want to wake you. I'll page him for you."

I'm beyond excited. My future wife is going to pull through. In time, we'll be able to put this tragedy behind us and move forward as a family. This is the best news I've heard in quite some time. There will be no more game playing for me. It's time to shoot straight from now on. I owe it to my sons and Sheena to be straight-forward and abandon the games. Additionally, I owe it to myself to not have the stress of all of the scheming and plotting on my shoulders. Stress has taken down many people who are much stronger than me.

"Thanks. Is it possible for me to see Ms. Mills? If so, what room is she in?" I inquire.

The nurse tells me what room she's in and I

start to run down the hallway to her room, but then I catch myself. How lame would I be to pop into Sheena's room with no balloons or anything? I'd be the worst fiancé ever. I have to at least get her a card. I remember seeing a gift shop downstairs, so I jump on the elevator to get balloons and a card. I quickly grab what I need, pay for it, and head right back upstairs. I make it to Sheena's room and I pause to take a deep breath before I walk in. I really don't know what to expect from her. Will she be weak or upset with me for shooting her? I guess I'm about to find out right now. I open the door and see a doctor standing at her bedside.

"Sorry, doctor. I didn't know you were in here. The lady at the nurse's station told me that I could come in. I wouldn't have barged in if I had known," I utter.

The doctor turns around and doesn't even acknowledge that I said anything. Instead, he just walks out without saying a word with his surgical mask on. He's pretty damn rude to supposedly be in a profession that's intended to help people. I wonder why he has his mask on. I would expect for him to have introduced himself since he's not the doctor from last night. Maybe Sheena's immune system is very weak and he didn't want to breathe on her. Shoot, it would have been nice if he would have told me something. I don't know if I should walk over to Sheena or not, or if I need a surgical mask.

Oh well, I walk over to Sheena's bed and her eyes are closed. I stand over her and marvel at her beauty. It's amazing how beautiful she is even in her weakened condition. I grab her hand and caress it gently. Then, I lean forward and kiss her on her forehead.

To my surprise, Sheena isn't sleeping. She was just resting her eyes. My baby gives me a warm smile. I smile back as I continue rubbing her hand.

"I'm glad you're here. I didn't want to be here alone," Sheena says.

"You know I'm here for you. You don't ever have to worry about that. They wouldn't let me see you when you initially got out of surgery, so I slept in the family room," I state.

"I knew you would stay the night. Too bad they didn't let you stay with me, but I was out of it anyway, so I guess it wouldn't have mattered," Sheena speaks.

"Yeah, I'm here now and you'll be fine they say, so that's all that matters now," I reply.

"Right, I'll be fine in no time. I'm sorry for coming in the house instead of letting you handle the situation. I almost got myself killed because I was too impatient to wait," Sheena confesses.

"No, it wasn't your fault. It was mine. I should have been more on point with my shooting. I was reckless and almost killed you," I respond. "I apologize."

"I think it's safe to say that we are both

culpable for the events that have transpired lately, but we have to place some of the blame on those two idiots Kevin and Eric. They went way too far and we had to do what we had to do to protect ourselves," Sheena verbalizes.

"Yes, they definitely took things to the extreme. I can understand being upset, but to try to kill us was out of this world ridiculous," I utter.

"Right, I agree. Where are the boys? Are they okay?" Sheena asks.

"The boys are fine. Ilesha took them home with her. She'll be back with them soon. She told me to call her when I had some news, so I guess that means I should give her a holla," I answer.

"Good, I'm glad the boys are good. I hope they didn't have to see me all bloody and carried out on the stretcher," Sheena conveys.

"No, we kept them pretty shielded from all that happened. They have no clue as to what transpired. They're oblivious to everything, but you could tell they miss you," I assure.

"You know I miss them already too. They almost lost me forever," Sheena speaks as a tear trickles down her cheek.

I reply, "I know you do. You're such a mom. Always missing her kids. Well, they aren't going to lose you, so don't be upset about something that hasn't happened."

"I'll always be a mom and they'll always be my babies. Even when they're grown and have families of their own," Sheena reports.

"Is that a woman thing? Oh yeah, what did the doctor say?" I ask.

"It's definitely a woman thing, so you'd ever understand. I don't know what he said. He was standing over me with a pillow as I was waking up and was mumbling something. I was quite groggy, so I really don't know what his deal was. Next thing I knew, you were standing in here," Sheena explains.

"Damn, I would've liked to speak to him, but I was so excited to see you that I let him slide out. Plus, he seemed to be in a rush to leave. He wasn't friendly like the doctor who spoke to us last night," I communicate.

As Sheena and I are chatting, there's a subtle knock at the door. We both look over at the door and see Dr. Cooper coming through. He's the doctor who operated on Sheena last night and informed us that she was going to pull through.

"Good afternoon Ms. Mills. Glad to see that you're awake. You were sleeping like a baby when I stopped through early this morning," says the doctor.

"I just want to thank you for saving my life doctor. I'm grateful that God worked his miracles through your hands last night," Sheena states.

"Yeah, we can't thank you enough doc. You worked a miracle for sure," I say. "You saved our family."

"I'm glad I was able to save the day. Don't thank me too much because Ms. Mills has a lot of fight in her. She was a soldier in surgery. She fought hard to stay alive and it worked because she's still here today," Dr. Cooper replies.

"Thanks doctor for being so kind. That's encouraging and I'll need all the motivation I can get to fully recover from this," Sheena comments.

"I agree. Being sensitive at a time like this is important. I'm glad you were her doctor last night and are here today because that other doctor seemed to not care one bit," I mention.

Dr. Cooper asks, "You do know that it's part of my job to be sensitive during troubling times? Who's the other doctor that you mentioned?"

"It's good to know that soft skills are still required. The doctor who was just in here moments before you walked in. He was standing over Sheena when I walked in. He wasn't very nice and left without giving me an update. I don't know what his problem was," I answer.

"He must be having a bad day cause he was standing over me mumbling something. He seemed normal from what I remember, but I was still kinda out of it," Sheena voices.

Dr. Cooper has a very confused look on his face. He's shaking his head while Sheena and I tell him about the other doctor. Why does he look so befuddled? He knows that everyone's not personable like he is. What's the likelihood that the doctor who just left isn't mean to everybody he encounters? My guess is slim to none.

"Doctor is everything okay? Are you going to be alright?" Sheena asks.

"Oh yeah, I'm fine, but I am a little interested in who this other doctor is. No physician should treat his patients like that," Dr. Cooper speaks.

"I feel the same way. I'm in the customer service industry and I know good customer service goes a long way and is very important to business," I convey.

"What field of customer service are you in? By chance, did you catch the doctor's name?" Dr. Cooper inquires.

"I own a nightclub called In the Mix. Unfortunately, I never got the doctor's name. Like I said, he was in and out and we didn't speak at all," I reply.

The doctor replies, "In the Mix. I love that place. I've been there a time or two to say the least. Many good memories there. Your people know how to make a good stiff drink. Anyway, that's real strange about the other doctor."

"What's strange about the other doctor?" Sheena asks.

"Well, I'm the only doctor working this floor and I'm actually your doctor, so I don't get why another physician was in your room," he answers. "I didn't ask anyone to check on you. Very strange."

"What are you getting at doc? What are you

implying?" I ask.

"Right, who was in here?" Sheena replies.

"I may be saying nothing. What did the doctor look like?" asks Dr. Cooper.

I answer Dr. Cooper's question, "The other doctor had on a surgical mask and most of his face was obscured, so I can't really provide a great description of him. However, I can tell you that he's a brown skinned African American male about six feet tall. I don't even know the texture of his hair because he had on a doctor's cap. I was able to see his eyes and they were light brown."

His facial expressions tell me that he's growing more concerned with every detail I utter. I hate to be the bearer of bad news, but I'm just stating what I know. Dr. Cooper tells us that there aren't any African American doctors working at the hospital that he's aware of.

"So, who was that guy and why was he in my room? How did he even get in here?" Sheena asks angrily.

"That's what we need to find out Ms. Mills. Please don't get yourself worked up about this. We'll get to the bottom of it. I promise," assures Dr. Cooper.

"Sheena, I'll definitely get to the bottom of this. Not now, but right now," I voice.

I wonder if that doctor is still on the floor. I walk out of Sheena's room to see if I can find the man who was just in here. I peer out of the room to the left and then to the right. Fortunately, I see the doctor who was in Sheena's room down the hall, so I scurry down the hall to talk to him. As I walk with purpose down the hallway, two nurses walk in front of me while carting a patient. I have to wait for them to pass by. I call out to the doctor to get his attention, but he quickly looks over his shoulder at me and heads for the staircase.

Damn, I have to catch up to him! Why won't these nurses get out of my way? I'm all for patient care, but I don't think the hallway is the place for it. I decide to squeeze pass them in the hallway and make my way to the staircase.

I'm in the staircase and I don't know if the doctor went up to the above floors or down to one of the ones below. I pause for a second to see if I can hear him walking up or down the stairs. I don't hear anything, so I call out to the doctor, but he doesn't respond. Thankfully, I hear some movement down below, so I take the stairs immediately and swiftly.

Why does it seem like this guy is trying to avoid me? What kind of doctor doesn't answer when he's being called. I can't wait to catch up to him. While I proceed down the stairs, I hear the sound of a door opening. The doctor must have exited the staircase to another floor. When I get down the next flight of stairs, I see a door closing on the second floor, so I go to it.

I get through the door and see the doctor

standing at the nurse's station. I'm livid from him avoiding me at this point. I go straight to the nurse's station and approach the doctor.

"Excuse me doctor, but why are you avoiding me? Don't you know that's extremely rude?" I ask sternly as I grab his arm to turn him around.

The doctor turns around from my tug at his arm and we are standing face to face. He's no longer wearing his surgical mask and his face is fully exposed. I'm confused as I look him in his eyes.

"Don't grab me man. You're crazy! I'm not a doctor, so when I heard you calling out for a doctor I didn't respond," he voices angrily.

I respond in an embarrassed fashion, "I apologize sir. I thought you were someone else. When I saw your lab coat, I just assumed you were a doctor. You were down the hall when I saw you, so I couldn't tell you weren't who I was seeking."

"Oh, I understand. The lab coat gets people all the time. I'm just a lab technician, but I wish I did make the big bucks like the doctors do. You must be pretty angry at that doctor to wanna grab his arm. I'm glad I'm not him," the lab technician states jokingly.

"Yeah, I am pretty upset. Again, I apologize for the case of mistaken identity. I was kinda peeved that you were ignoring me," I utter.

"No problem man. Take it easy. Sorry, I had you walk down all those steps," says the lab technician.

I walk off confused. I knew when the lab technician turned around that he wasn't the same person who was in Sheena's room when I initially walked in. I was only able to see the eyes of the man who was standing at her bed and the lab technician's eyes were not the same ones I stared into. Who in the hell was that guy?

I stroll to the elevator on that floor and take it back to Sheena's floor. I stop at the nurse's station to ask them about the doctor who was making rounds on that floor. I tell them that the man was African American and was brown skinned, but they have no clue as to who I'm referring to.

"No sir. There aren't any doctors here fitting that description. Sorry, but the person couldn't have been a doctor," replies the nurse.

I leave their station and go back to Sheena's room. When I walk in, I notice Sheena's doctor is gone, but Ilesha and Rachel are in here with the boys.

"Hey," says Ilesha and Rachel simultaneously.

"Whatever," I reply curtly.

"Well, the hell with you too. With Sheena doing well, there's no reason for you to be so smug. Especially to us. We haven't done anything to you," Ilesha speaks. "If anything, we should be mad at your ass for not calling us."

Rachel chimes in, "I understand that you're under a lot of pressure from Sheena being shot and all, but Ilesha's right, there's no need to treat us poorly. We're only here to help. I think you owe us an apology."

"You're right ladies. You two haven't done anything to warrant me being rude to you. It's really this entire situation that has me upset and a bit unlike myself. It seems like when you get through one set of bullshit, there's another boatload of bullshit waiting for you," I verbalize.

Ilesha states, "You're right, but this is the end of it. Those two assholes Kevin and Eric are both dead, so now the bullshit stops. The nonsense is over and now only good times rest ahead."

"I wish that were the case, but the bullshit isn't over from what it seems," I reply.

"What are you talking about Sage? What's the issue now? Why are you so bent out of shape?" Rachel inquires.

"The bullshit going on is that there was a doctor in here when I first came in this afternoon to check on Sheena and now he's nowhere to be found," I say.

Ilesha chimes in before I finish explaining, "Okay, so that's normal. Please get to the bullshit. Don't nobody got all day for you to be dancing around the meat of the story."

"Damn, you know you are rude and impatient as hell," I reply.

"Well, out with it then!" Ilesha returns.

"Back to what I was saying before I was so

rudely interrupted. So, there was a doctor in here standing over Sheena with a pillow in his hand. He sped outta here as soon as I walked in. Of course that is suspect in itself, but nobody in the hospital can verify that the guy is even a doctor. It appears that the guy doesn't really work here," I explain.

"So, what are you implying? Are you implying that someone's trying to hurt Sheena again?" Rachel inquires.

"Well, even if it's not that, something doesn't sound right. Damn, fake doctors, pillows, and nobody knows the guy," Ilesha voices.

"This is really frightening. I thought this drama died with Kevin and Eric, but clearly I was wrong," Sheena speaks.

"Sister, don't get too worked up over this. It could all just be a crazy coincidence. Sage saw him, so he can just provide a description of him to the hospital official and I'm sure we'll find the guy," Rachel asserts optimistically.

I reply, "It's not quite that simple. The guy was wearing a surgical mask, so I didn't see his face. Unfortunately, all I could see was his eyes. They were brown, big, and slightly sunken in."

"Damn. That would have been great to have a look at his face. You'd at least be able to give a description of the person to the cops," Ilesha remarks.

"I can't believe that someone still wishes to harm Sheena. I'm even more shocked that someone was brazen enough to come to the hospital to hurt her. I'm so disgusted with the actions of mankind today. We need healing," Rachel narrates.

"What's even worse is that we have nowhere to turn for a suspect. I don't feel safe and don't want to be alone," says Sheena.

I voice, "I won't leave you alone. I'll be with you or have someone here with you until you're released. I promise."

"Yes, sister. Don't worry about that. We'll be sure to have you protected. We need to contact the authorities in the meantime. They may put a guard at your door twenty-four hours a day," Rachel mentions.

"That's a good idea. I'll let the hospital personnel know that we need an officer here," I inform.

I leave the room and go to the third floor to the hospital's security office. When I get to the office, there are several men and women in the office. I'm greeted immediately by one of them and they ask me if I need any help. I begin telling the security personnel what took place earlier in Sheena's room. They are astonished to find that someone is potentially impersonating a doctor in this hospital.

I'm both shocked and relieved that they are taking my claims seriously because I have no proof to support my claim. They ask me several questions about the incident. For example, they ask what room Sheena's in, what took place in the room, and what the guy looked like. I answer their questions honestly and to the best of my ability. After that, one of the officers walks with me back to Sheena's room to talk to her for a few.

CHAPTER 3
Sage's Perspective

The security guard comes to Sheena's room and asks her the same questions he asked me. She tells him that she doesn't remember much because of the medication she was under. She also tells him that she thought she was dreaming until I confirmed what she thought she was dreaming was actually real. She says a man was standing at her bedside and placed a pillow over her face momentarily. The next thing she knew, he was gone and I was in the room asking her what the doctor said. Sheena also says that she can't give a description of him because she was out of it and his face was partially covered.

I ask, "Are all these questions really necessary? Couldn't you use what I told you to cast your investigation?"

He replies, "Seeing how she is the patient of

the hospital and the intended victim, I need to talk to her to file a formal complaint and get this stuff on record. We have to keep patients safe at all times and I need her account of what transpired. I hope you find that to be sufficient and adequate as to why I came to talk to Miss Mills."

I comment, "I understand sir. I just didn't want her to be disturbed again if it wasn't absolutely necessary. She has had an awfully long night and afternoon. We almost lost her and I just wanted her to rest without being interrupted. I apologize if I came off a bit abrupt and rude as that wasn't my intention."

"I understand. We've seen this sort of thing a million times. We know family members can be agitated and upset. Sometimes the frustrations and uncertainties of situations make people act uncharacteristically. I'm guilty of it myself, so I totally understand what you are going through. I'm an official of the hospital and I'm here to help whenever I can," the security guard expresses.

Ilesha remarks, "That's nice to say, but this must be a bullshit hospital if someone can just parade around as a doctor and go from room to room without obstruction. That mystery doctor could have raped Sheena, knocked her out, or even killed her. If it weren't for Sage coming into the room, that guy probably would have suffocated Sheena."

Rachel speaks, "She's right sir. This incident doesn't look good for your security team. All the patients in here are vulnerable."

"I assure you that you are in great hands. We'll get to the bottom of this right now. I have my guy in the security office going over the security footage from your floor right now. He'll have something for me any minute. It's good that we know the exact time to run the security camera back to. It saves a lot of time," he states as he looks toward Sheena.

Moments later, the security officer's phone rings and he answers it. The guy on the other end tells him that he has viewed the security tapes during the time when the unknown suspect was in Sheena's room. Unfortunately, he tells that he's unable to see the guy's face in video because it is obscured. Furthermore, he informs him that he's followed this guy on camera throughout the hospital and can't catch a glimpse of his face anywhere from within the perimeters of the hospital walls. Also to our dismay, he says the guy's not seen driving through the parking lot of the hospital either. The guy comes strolling up from off camera and enters the hospital and goes straight to Sheena's room.

The security guard exits the room and heads back to the office, so he can view the tapes himself. He wants to make sure that the guy didn't miss anything valuable. He even states that he'll try to get security tapes from other businesses in the area to see where the dude may have walked from and hopefully he'll be able to get a glimpse of the guy's face from one of their cameras. At some point, God had to have his face uncovered.

Needless to say, we are less than happy about the findings here today. We were hoping that this guy's face would be seen on tape somewhere, so we can start to get a handle on this. It's unsettling to know that someone is out there trying to kill Sheena, but we have no idea who it is, why they want to hurt her, or when they will strike again. All we know for now is that Sheena can't be left alone, not even for a minute, since this hospital is so easy to infiltrate. For all we know, the next time the person could disguise himself as the cleaning staff or as a person who delivers food from the cafeteria to the patients. All of those people have unimpeded access to the patients' rooms and no one would think anything of it.

About 10 minutes after the security guard leaves, Officer Mosely walks into Sheena's hospital room. We are totally surprised that he's here, but we are also extremely glad that he is. We will be able to tell him what happened and hopefully get some police protection for Sheena while she's confined to the hospital. We pleasantly greet the detective for coming to visit and for his diligent efforts at Sheena's house last night. He was very meticulous in his investigation and was very sensitive to our needs during such a precarious situation.

I say, "Detective Mosely, I'm surprised to see you here. We didn't know you made hospital calls. That's nice of you to check up on Sheena and the rest of us. It really means a lot. Most cops would have forgotten about us back at the house, but not you. We knew you were special."

Officer Mosely replies, "I wish someone would tell my wife that I'm special. She treats me like I'm a miscreant. Just kidding, but on a more serious note, I've been trying to contact you all afternoon Sage."

"Really? What's so urgent that you've been trying to contact me all afternoon?" I inquire.

"There's a new development in Sheena's case that I wanted to make you aware of, so I called several times and also texted you to let you know what's going on," Officer Mosely states.

"I apologize. My phone's battery died and I had no way to charge it. I've been up here all night waiting to hear something about Sheena, so charging the phone wasn't really urgent. I wasn't going to leave to get a charger. Here it is, I'm thinking you are here about what happened last night," I say.

"Well, what's the new development officer?" asks Sheena eagerly.

"There sure are a hell of a lot of new developments going on right now. It's too damn much for my liking. We have to get to the bottom of this now!" says Ilesha.

"New developments here? Did you guys want to tell me that Miss Mills is clearly doing well?" asks Officer Mosely.

"Yeah, she's doing well as you can see, but that's not why we would have been contacting you," explains Rachel.

I chime in, "I wish it were for good news, but unfortunately contacting you would not have been for that. It seems that there's a fake doctor roaming the hospital and he even attempted to suffocate Sheena a few hours back. It was only by the grace of God that I walked in the room and precluded his plan. I'm sick to my stomach that he was able to get out of here without me stopping him. The bastard even had on a surgical mask, so I couldn't see his face, but I recognize those brown sunken eyes anywhere."

"I'd be lying if I said I was surprised because I'm not. That's the news that I wanted to tell you over the phone when I was calling," Officer Mosely speaks.

"What's the news?" I ask.

"I thought it was strange that we found a garage door opener on Eric Burns' dead body last night. He had nothing else on him other than that garage door opener and the gun that we pulled his prints off of. I began to ask myself why someone would bring a garage door opener to try to kill someone. For that reason, I decided to hit the garage door opener button and I heard

Ms. Mills' garage door open up," Detective Mosely says.

"Why would that be strange? Doesn't that just eliminate the question of how they were able to enter the house to begin with?" I inquire.

He answers, "The presence of the garage door opener definitely answered the question of how they entered the premises, but it also left me with another question."

"And that question was?" I ask.

"Well, I thought back to the night the intruder broke into Ms. Mills' house. The guy, who we assumed was one of her two ex-boyfriends, broke in through the back door by breaking the glass. If he had the garage door opener and could get in that way, it wouldn't make sense for him to enter through the back door," Detective Mosely explains.

I suggest, "I get it, but it is possible that he hadn't purchased it yet. It could have been an afterthought."

"I totally agree and my thinking took me in that direction initially, but it was still a question mark in my mind that I needed to answer, so I figured I'd have the prints pulled off of Eric Burns and Kevin Bailey. The prints I took from the night Ms. Mills was attacked in her home did not match any in our database. Now, what's even stranger is that when Kevin's and Eric's corpses were brought to the morgue, I had my guy run their prints versus the ones I collected off the floor the night Ms. Mills was attacked and they didn't match those prints either. At that point, it became painfully obvious that we have another suspect to worry about," he explains.

"You gotta be fucking kidding me!" I reply.

I don't tell Detective Mosely that I also had a huge question about the night Sheena was attacked too. Fortunately, he answered it for me without even knowing it. I couldn't figure out why Leslie didn't tell me about one of them breaking into Sheena's house that night. I was bewildered as to why Kevin kept Leslie in the loop about everything he and Eric were up to, but decided to leave that vicious attack out of the story. It's because it wasn't Kevin or Eric. Now, this new development is definitely something to be seriously concerned about, but I won't show it.

"So there really is another person out their trying to harm me! Well, I need to get out of this hospital because it's obviously too easy for someone to get at me here," Sheena states as she frantically moves the sheets to the side.

"Oh no Miss Mills, you'll be fine. I brought an officer with me who will be stationed outside of your door at all times. The only time he won't be there is when there's a shift change and you'll be well aware of that before it takes place. Had we known up front that Kevin and Eric weren't the suspects, we would have had someone stationed outside of your door to begin with. From all of the evidence we had, it really looked as if Kevin and Eric were the only suspects. Well, at least one of them," he remarks.

"Well, that's good to know. At least Sheena can sleep comfortably without worrying about being assaulted. The only problem now is finding out who this mystery man is. He has the upper hand because all he needs is for us to be vulnerable for one moment and we have no idea which way he's coming from," I reply.

"So, what do you suggest we do officer?" asks Sheena.

"All we can do for now is let the investigation process take place. I promise you that we'll take this guy down and put this issue to bed for good. Hopefully, Kevin and/or Eric solicited the help of one of their friends or family members. If so, we'll be able to track this guy down through cell phone records, interrogations, and other good old-fashioned police work," voices Officer Mosely.

"Sheena, you just worry about getting better and let them do their part to make sure you're safe. Don't worry about the boys. I'll make sure they're good to go along with Sage and Rachel. They need their mommy to be strong and up and running again," says Ilesha.

"I know they need me to be strong. I'll recover and be back better than ever from this. I know I can count on you guys to have my back. I want to give my boys a big hug right now but I'm still a little too weak to do that and don't want to overextend myself," Sheena verbalizes.

Officer Mosely stays another few minutes and then leaves. He says that he has other cases to work on and some leads to follow up pertaining to Sheena's case. He also wants to go to the hospital security headquarters and view the security tapes himself. He just wants to make sure that he covers all bases and doesn't miss anything pertinent to finding out who the felonious caper is. Rachel visits a little while longer, but eventually departs with the boys. We all agree that it's not beneficial to the boys to be cooped up in a hospital room all day long. They really don't need to see Sheena in such bad shape and besides there are a lot of germs they may be exposed to if they stay here. Sheena's mom is coming to town to see Sheena and pick up the boys. The boys will be spending some quality time with their grandmother at my house until Sheena's up and running.

Ilesha and I are here. We help comfort Sheena as much as possible. The doctor says she was lucky and she'll be up and running in no time. I still can't believe I shot and almost killed the love of my life. I've got to make better decisions and be more honest in my dealings. My underhandedness almost cost Sheena her life and my sons their mother. How could I have possibly explained to them what I did if she had perished? I keep trying not to blame myself, but it's really weighing on me.

We continue talking to Sheena for a while, but she eventually falls asleep. The medication they are giving her to cope with the pain has rendered her unconscious. Ilesha and I laugh at Sheena as she snores loudly. Ilesha is here and Sheena is asleep, so I decide to go home and take a shower. In addition, I need some fresh air because I've been at the hospital all night and day. I'm sure I've missed many calls too, so this will give me an opportunity to check up on some things. I definitely need to handle some important business related to getting the lounge back up and running.

I leave the hospital and head to the car. I get to the car and hook my phone up to the car charger. As soon as I power it on, it starts chiming incessantly from messages. I see several messages from Detective Mosely in my text messages inbox. Many of the texts are from friends of mine who heard what happened to Sheena and are checking with me to make sure she's okay. I reply to several of them and proceed to pull out of the hospital parking lot.

As I drive home, I check my voicemail messages. My mom and several other family members have called because they too heard about what happened last night. I'll call them back when I get home. I continue checking my voicemail messages and hear one message that's very startling. It's a man speaking in a very low and sinister tone. I don't recognize his voice, but it doesn't matter because his message is crystal clear.

"I hope you don't think this shit is over bitch because it's not. This is only the beginning. Consider Sheena lucky. She was supposed to die today, but her luck is going to run out just like her breath is. It's only a matter of time before that bitch is filled with maggots," says the voice on my voicemail.

Shit! This person is clearly a lunatic. I'll be damned if something else happens to Sheena while I'm still breathing. Ain't no way in hell anymore harm will come to her head. I call Detective Mosely, so I can inform him of the message I received.

"This is Detective Mosely," he answers.

"Hi, Detective Mosely. This is Sage McMillan from the hospital. I just turned my phone on and listened to some of my voice messages. It appears that one of the messages is from the individual who was in Sheena's hospital room earlier today. He was basically threatening her saying she got lucky and there's more to come. I felt it necessary to contact you as soon as possible. I don't know if this can help with your investigation, but I figured I would let you decide that," I say.

"I'm sorry to hear that. I don't want you to be alarmed because like I said earlier, we'll figure it all out and get this guy off the street. Yes, we can use the tape of the voicemail as potential evidence going forward. You never know, we may have to do some voice analysis to put one more nail in the coffin and catch this creep. I would love to hear the voicemail," Officer Mosely states.

"Yes, I figured it may help with the investigation at some point. If you want to listen to it, hold on for a moment. I'll call my voicemail and then conference you in on the line. That way you'll be able to hear it for yourself," I suggest.

"That's a great idea. I'll hold and wait for you to conference me in," he utters.

I put the detective on hold and access my voicemail again. I cue up the message and join Detective Mosely to the current line. Now, we both listen to the voicemail together. He is just alarmed as I am. He also remarks about how sinister the man who made the voicemail message sounds. He wants me to come down to the station, so they can get a copy of the voicemail and for me to put it on file that someone's harassing me. I decide not to wait to go to the police station and head straight there to handle this order of business in the investigation.

Detective Mosely is at the station when I arrive. An analyst promptly gets a recording of my voicemail, I provide a statement, and depart to go home. I get home and sit on the couch for a moment to take in all that has transpired last night and this afternoon. It's a man's job to protect his family and I vow that. I will do just that. I know one thing, Detective Mosely better find this guy before I do because if he doesn't, I'm going to kill him. I can't live with knowing that there's a constant threat against my family out there somewhere.

I just want to know who this nut case is. That's the nerve-racking part. Just knowing that any random guy on the street could be the person is unsettling. I finally jump up off of the couch after a few minutes of deep cogitation and head for the shower. My clothes are soggy and I feel sticky and unlike myself. This shower is going to do my body good for sure. My shower is as refreshing as I intended it to be. When I exit the shower, I dry off and lie across my bed. I decide to make a few calls to see where things are as far as the lounge is concerned. The drywall guys were supposed to be coming in today. Fortunately, they are on schedule, so that's one less thing for me to worry about. It seems that all things are in order with the lounge, so now I just kick back. Without even planning it, I fall into a deep sleep.

CHAPTER 4
Sage's Perspective

It's been three weeks since Sheena initially went into the hospital because I shot her. Her road to recovery was long, arduous, and slow, but she has made it through. I can say this has definitely been the longest three weeks of my life. I've had to juggle many things before in my life but the items I've been juggling the past three weeks are much more important than anything I've ever done before.

I've been juggling being a father almost by myself. Not to slight Ilesha, Rachel, or Sheena's mom for the help they gave me, but it still seemed like I was alone. Not to mention, my time has been split another way with getting In the Mix back up and running. Most importantly, I've been spending countless hours at the hospital with Sheena. I've even had to check in on her business from time to time just to make sure things were flowing as smoothly as they possibly could.

The good thing about the entire process is that the hospital juggling portion is finally over today. Sheena is leaving any moment now. Her recovery was better than what the doctors expected. I'm not surprised though, because she's the type of person who beats the odds. She's exceptional in all that she does, so why would this be any different?

Sheena has been ready to come home for at least two weeks, but the doctors would not allow it and personally, I didn't think she was ready to come home either. She's very excited about being able to leave the hospital today. Sheena's so impatient. She's upset that the doctor hasn't released her yet even though it's still 30 minutes before he said he would. I guess I can understand where she's coming from because I was the same way when I got shot. I didn't want to stay in the hospital for a night let alone three weeks. I never thought I would be able to share being shot with someone close to me, but one thing life has shown me is that we never know what to expect.

I wonder if Sheena's harboring any ill feelings towards me from shooting her. She has to know it was purely accidental and wouldn't have happened if she would have stayed outside of the house like the plan was to begin with. I'm sure if she's feeling some type of way about the incident, she'll let me know. Sheena isn't the type of person to hold how she's feeling back for too long. It would eat her up inside to do that.

Rachel and Ilesha are helping Sheena get dressed now. I'm downstairs waiting in the lobby with the boys, so I can get the car as soon as they call to let me know that she's being released. I wanted to stay in the room with them, but they wouldn't have it. I guess men can't be in the room with women while they're getting beautiful. You would think I wasn't sitting in the hospital for the last three weeks seeing Sheena at her worst. The funny thing is that her worst is more beautiful than most women's best. My future wife is naturally beautiful and doesn't need man-made adornments to make her beautiful.

Finally, I get a phone call from Rachel informing me that Sheena has been released and that they are on their way downstairs. I rush to the car to pull around to where she'll be released. I'm sitting in front of the hospital release area when my beautiful bride-to-be comes walking out beautifully, healthily, and confidently. I jump out of the car and zoom to her to give her a warm embrace.

"Damn Sage. If you hug Sheena any harder, you're going to break her ass. It's not like you haven't seen her. I know what it is. You were just tired of beating your dick and you know you're going to be able to get you some now.

That's why his ass is all excited," Ilesha jokes.

Rachel chimes, "Girl, you are so brazen. You'll say anything. You don't need to comment on Sage's sexual frustrations. We know he's been going through it lately."

"I can't believe you two are really having this conversation right here in front of me. Shit, I am standing here. You could at least spare my pride and have this conversation behind my back," I comment.

"Alright Ilesha. Leave him alone. He's been a soldier through this and hasn't bothered me. He's only been helpful, so we'll let him off the hook this time. But yeah, I'm sure his dick is blue as hell girl," says Sheena with a smirk on her face.

Ilesha remarks, "Girl, I bet his dick looks like a damn Smurf."

They start cracking up laughing at my expense. I know it's funny because even Rachel is laughing even though she's trying not to. I can't front. I'm laughing myself. This is the longest I've ever been without sex, but tonight is going to end the drought. I'm definitely giving Sheena all I have tonight. She'll fuck around and get pregnant after this load I'm going to leave in her.

Sheena gets into the car under her own power. She really didn't need me to pull the car up, but I did it as a courtesy. She's moving very well and is like her old self again. She has the look of strength in her eyes and a pop in her step. She certainly has her swagger back and I'm glad to see it. We all are in my vehicle and are heading back to my house while we converse.

Rachel states, "Okay sister. Now when you get back to the house, I want you to take things easy. Don't try to overdo it. You know you still aren't one hundred percent yet, so don't go overboard."

"Honey please! I'm fine and I don't need to sit my ass down. I'm ready to run now. Besides, I have a wedding to plan. You know I wasn't just sitting in the hospital doing nothing. Another six months and I'll be married," Sheena speaks assertively.

"Now you know, I don't think that's a good idea. You shouldn't take on all of those tasks at one time. Your body has to adjust back to its normal proceedings. Planning a wedding, parenting, and running your business after something as traumatic as being shot is not the best idea. It's not what the doctor ordered," Rachel utters in a concerned tone.

Ilesha voices her opinion, "Rachel, now you know Sheena is headstrong. If she wants to do it, she's going to do it. Girl, you just wasting your breath trying to talk her out of it. In fact, you're just making her want to do it more. Sheena, I'm on your side. If you think you can do it, I know you can do it."

"Thanks Rachel for being so concerned about me. It really means a lot, but I'm fine. Really, I'm fine. Ilesha, I know you got my back girl," I mention.

"Girl, I have your back forever and three days. You never have to question that, but the question is if Sage can handle a wedding in six months. We know he ain't working," Ilesha tells.

I speak, "If all I have to do is write a check to be considered ready for the wedding, then sure, I'm ready right now. The few thousand won't break the bank."

"Well excuse me!" Ilesha says.

"You are excused," I say while clearing my throat.

"We're planning my wedding! We're planning my wedding!" says Sheena in a singing manner.

Ilesha and Rachel join Sheena with the planning a wedding singing. I just shake my head and let them have their moment. I'm looking forward to my wedding day as well, but not to the extent that they are. I mean, I'm sure it's going to be fun and special but I'm not going to be singing songs about it in the car.

The rest of the ride back to my house is fairly smooth and enjoyable. It's almost like she never got hurt. This ride reminds me of the many times we have ridden together. Everything is all good. At first, I questioned if we should all ride home together once Sheena was released from the hospital, but I'm not questioning it anymore because it all makes sense now. I believe we'll all remember this ride home for the rest of our lives. It's one of those memorable moments that people never forget. It's also symbolic of how we'll be from this point moving forward. Sheena, Ilesha, Rachel, the boys, and me. That's the team from this day forward. I might as well accept it now because I know there's no way I'm going to be able to pry Sheena away from her girls. As the saying goes, "if you can't beat them, join them."

Sheena decided that she's no longer going to live at her former residence. There's just too many mixed memories from that place that she wants to forget about. I don't blame her because I wouldn't want to live somewhere where all of that drama happened. It's not even my place and the thought of two people being murdered there is still really quite unbelievable. To be honest, I don't want Sheena or my sons in that place. Just the thought of that night makes me shake my head. I can only imagine how she would feel stepping over the exact location where her two former lovers were shot dead. It's the same house where she was attacked by an unknown assailant and to make matters worse, it's the same house where she was unfortunately shot by me and almost lost her life. I wouldn't expect anyone to want to relive those thoughts and emotions on a daily basis. That could drive someone crazy if they weren't already scarred for life.

I'm not the least bit upset that she's not going back there. I want her and the boys here with me because that's how a family should be. Families should be together as one under the same roof in my mind. Also, Sheena and the boys being here allows me to keep a better eye on them. I have a state-of-the-art security system and I'll also be here also to make sure they are in safe hands. It's a man's job to protect his family and I truly believe that. It's a job that I don't have the luxury of being subpar or failing at.

We pull up to the house and the ladies join arm in arm and joyfully prance inside the house. I carry the boys in behind them. Everyone gathers in the living room and then I walk back outside to the car to grab Sheena's belongings from the hospital to bring them inside. Sheena has clothes for days. Why would she have needed all of these clothes in the hospital? It's not like she was going anywhere.

Later in the day, I'm in the kitchen making my world-famous lasagna for dinner when the doorbell rings. I'm expecting company, but I still don't take any chances when answering the door, so I grab my gun and approach my front door. On the way to the door, Rachel is already attempting to open it. She hasn't even asked who it is. I know I live in a great neighborhood with very expensive houses, but this is still Washington D.C., our nation's capital, and we have to be careful because of it. Not to mention, there's still someone out there who chooses to cause Sheena harm.

"Rachel! Don't open the door! You can't open the door without checking to see who it is!"

I yell.

"Sage, you live in a great neighborhood. No one is coming here to bother us. They wouldn't make it a block without a police officer catching them," Rachel replies.

I say, "Don't think that for sure. Naiveté is what a lot of people prey on. That's how they catch you slipping when people think certain things don't happen in certain neighborhoods. It gives us a false sense of security and makes us more vulnerable none the less. We can't get caught slipping because it could be the matter of life or death."

"I totally understand that. It won't happen again," Rachel states.

"Sage, you are right. Once I saw her going for the door, I pulled my knife out just in case," Ilesha utters.

"Well, I guess we would have been alright. I know firsthand how deft you are with that knife," I say as I rub my neck where she cut me.

The girls start laughing, but I don't. I don't laugh because I don't see anything funny about having a knife pulled on me. Not that I'm upset or anything because I'm not. As far as I'm concerned, that's water under the bridge. To some degree, I have to admit that I deserved it. I attempted to break up their sisterhood and it came back on me. I have scars as proof. I walk over to the door with my gun drawn.

"Who is it?" I call out.

"It's me. Monster," the person replies.

I open the door, to let him in. Monster walks in and I introduce him to the girls. I've known Monster for years. We started college together at Howard University back in the day. Monster is about 6 feet 5 inches tall and raves about 260 pounds and is all muscle. Monster used to beat up everybody in college if they messed with him.

Other than that, he's a very pleasant guy. He is so tough and dependable that I hired him on at In the Mix when I took over. He's been down with me ever since and he has never let me down.

"You look very familiar Mr. Monster. I know Monster isn't your government name," voices Rachel.

"Yeah, you definitely look familiar. Oh, I know why. He's old boy from the lounge," Ilesha voices.

"That is right. He's the security guard who threw the girl out that stripped down butt naked at the Halloween party. Your name isn't Monster; your name is Devon," Rachel reports.

I ask, "Baby, you remember Monster, right?"

"No honey, I don't remember Monster. I remember Devon. Hi Devon," Sheena words.

"Sup Sheena? Are you feeling any better?" Devon asks.

"Ain't much up. And yes, I feel fine. I feel strong. Thank you for asking," Sheena responds.

"I'm glad you two know each other because that's going to make this even easier," I say.

"Why you acting like you didn't know that I know Devon? Make what go even easier Sage?" Sheena asks.

I answer, "I didn't know if you remembered him or not. Well as you remember, Devon used to be on my security team at the lounge and since it caught fire, he obviously hasn't been working for me. I figure we can both benefit from our current predicament. Devon is out of work and you need someone to look after you until this madness is settled, so I hired him to keep an eye on you. This way he has employment and you're protected. Everyone wins here."

"Sage, I don't know about a bodyguard. This is a little extreme," Sheena replies.

"Girl, please. You crazy as hell! You better take the damn bodyguard before ya ass end up dead like Kevin and Eric," Ilesha orders.

"Yes, Sheena. Ilesha has a point. Some crazy person is out there trying to harm you and you don't know who it is, so a bodyguard just makes sense," Rachel remarks.

"Okay, damn. I don't need you all ganging up on me. You guys must care about me a lot to want me heavily protected. I won't refuse any protection. Devon, thanks for your help. I appreciate it," Sheena says.

"Sheena, you are like Michelle Obama or something. Real first lady shit. Got ya own security detail and shit. I ain't mad at cha," Ilesha jokes.

"Bet! I'm glad that's settled. Sheena, no matter what you said, I was still going to have Devon watch after you. I wasn't giving in on this one, so I'm glad you agreed," I voice.

"I think I can really get used to the idea of having my own personal bodyguard. Trust me, you won't hear another peep of resistance from me again Sage," Sheena utters gloatingly.

I reply, "Cool, because I don't wanna hear your damn mouth anyway. I hope you don't start walking around with the big head from having Monster watching over you."

"No, honey. I won't have a big head about having a bodyguard, but I might about this wedding though! Oh, you can bet your bottom dollar that I have a big head about it," Sheena voices confidently.

"Yes, a wedding is definitely a reason to be feeling very good about yourself. A union of man and woman is the ultimate relationship goal," Rachel comments.

"Hell yeah, marriage will give you the opportunity to be nasty as hell with your man and not feel guilty about it," Ilesha states.

I take Monster to the porch with me to discuss some specific duties that he'll have while protecting Sheena. Although I need to make him aware of my expectations for him, I escort him to the porch, so I don't have to hear all of that girl talk that Sheena, Ilesha, and Rachel are having. Monster and I talk for about thirty minutes. He has an understanding of what to do and not to do, so he departs. I go back in the house and head straight to my man room with the boys while Sheena continues to converse with her friends.

CHAPTER 5
Sheena's Attacker's Perspective

It amazes me how people speak on what they would do in situations that they've never been in. For example, people say if someone breaks into their home they would shoot them on sight or beat them down. However, the truth of the matter is that you don't know what you would do. You may be the person who freezes up and goes into shock when you see the intruder. Now, don't get me wrong, you could also be the person who really does stand up and become the hero. All I'm saying is that one never knows what they will do until they are put in that situation.

Look at me. I never thought that I would be trying to kill someone, but I am. I know one thing and it's that this is not my fault. I'm the victim here even though many people may not think so. I really don't care what people think anyway. I'm a man on a mission and I will complete it. Not only will I complete what I have to do, I'm going to get away with it. That's right. No jail cells for me. Nope, no dropping the soap.

I wasn't always this way. I was never angry. In fact, I was the guy who was always known for being happy go lucky and very cheerful. All of my friends wanted to be around me because I would be the life of the party. Unfortunately, things are different because I haven't been happy for a very long time. It's been years since I've really been happy.

The good thing is that I know happiness is right around the corner. As soon as I'm able to make sure Sheena suffers, then the happy days will be here again. I'll find solace in knowing that Sheena is not well off. I'm growing more infuriated each day that she's still here breathing the same air that I breathe. That bitch has to die and not die a natural death, but die and suffer by my hands and my doing. I'll be sure to make that bitch die slowly.

A lot of the times people say things are personal or things are business. Well in this instance, this is strictly personal, but I will make it my business to make sure the score is settled. I'm disgusted that she's still here. Shit, I'm beginning to think that Sheena has 9 lives like a cat. That's okay though because even a cat runs out of lives and so will she. It's apparent that luck is on her side, but fate is on mine. We all know that fate trumps luck in the end.

I realize now that it's just going to take more effort than I initially intended it to. Sheena and Sage are a bit more savvy than many people may know. I tried to killed Sheena at her home and the hospital, but was unsuccessful on both attempts. Not to mention, Eric and Kevin also attempted to kill Sheena and they were unsuccessful. Those damn fuckers even lost their lives behind it. I definitely won't lose my life behind this. The only one dying is Sheena.

They say when you experience love, your days are always bright and euphoric. I know that's true because when I had love in my life, I never experienced a dreary day. It was like no matter what was going on, it could never bring me off my high horse. I was riding high on cloud nine.

Love is truly a motivating factor. Love will have you walk 100 miles in the rain or stay up all night working on a project. When you love someone or something you will do your very best make sure that the thing or person you love is protected. Unfortunately, losing the thing that you love brings about feelings of emptiness and depression. That's where I'm at now and that's why she now has to die. Maybe I'll even send Sage video footage of me torturing Sheena.

The funny thing is that love and hate are very closely related. They both can take control of your day-to-day thoughts and actions. Love and hate are also both very motivating factors. The love of someone or the hate you have for someone can both drive you to places that you've never been. I'd rather be driven by love, but that's not the case for me anymore. Hate is what drives me now and I am focused and determined on my mission of making Sheena no longer breathe.

That's the only way to set things right. I know two wrongs don't make a right, but they damn sure make things even. I'm definitely all for equality. I'm a firm believer in an eye for an eye and a tooth for a tooth. If someone hurts me or mine, I will hurt them equally as bad or worse. You can't do dirt and not expect for karma to visit your doorstep. I am karma.

I'm going to lay low for a little bit before I make my next move. I'm sure after my missed opportunity at the hospital, Sheena will have the police watching over her, but when the time is right, I'll have my way with her. I have to plan my assault meticulously. If the police aren't on full alert about Sheena's predicament, I know Sage is. That's okay because I have the element of surprise on my side. They don't know when or where I'm going to attack. If I wanted to, I could go ring the doorbell right now, but I know I'd be met with opposition.

Sage's house is exquisite to say the least. I need to complete several more stakeouts before I'll be comfortable accessing his house to get to Sheena if that's what it takes. I see his former security guard just arrived. I think his name is Monster. Yeah, that's it. I figure Sage is going to hire Monster to protect Sheena. Monster won't be a problem for me to get past. I'm just glad that I'm sitting outside of Sage's place and saw him arrive. Now, I can plan what I'm going to do to him. Had I not seen him here today, I could have been caught off guard when making my move on Sheena. Chance favors the prepared mind and I'll be damned if I'm not prepared.

They've been inside long enough with nobody else coming in or out of Sage's house, so I guess this is my cue to leave. However, I'll be back and when it's time, I'll be bringing hell back with me. I drive away from Sage's house and head home. The real scheming begins now.

CHAPTER 6
Sheena's Perspective

"Girls, this dress doesn't look anything like how it looked on the internet. This online shopping for a wedding dress is killing my ass. You can't tell how anything really looks, feels, or fits until you've already paid your money for it. I'm not keeping this tired ass dress," I say.

Rachel speaks, "Yasss, I tend to agree with you on this one too. It's better than the other one you ordered, but it pales in comparison to the way they represented it on the internet. I wouldn't keep it either."

"Pales in comparison is like saying the dress we looked at on the web was a ten and this one is an eight. No, that's not it though. The dress we saw on the internet was a ten and this shit right here…this shit right here, is exactly that… Shit!" Ilesha voices.

"It is pretty bad girl. I wouldn't wear it and I'd send it back and demand a refund," Rachel states.

"Honey, no offense, but you know like Sheena and I do that your ass wouldn't send it back and demand a damn thing. You wouldn't wear it for sure, but your ass would just donate it to Good Will or something," Ilesha shoots back.

I start laughing and shaking my head in agreement with what Ilesha said. It's the truth because Rachel has done that in the past. She wouldn't make a fuss over some clothes to save her life. All she ever does is complain to us and never ruffles a feather. She just wants us to know that she vehemently disapproves of the dress I received.

"She's right. You know how you do girl," I say.

"Okay, she is, but you get my point. I'm just not in favor of the dress is all," Rachel utters.

Ilesha vocalizes aggressively, "Hell, I know I'm right. You two don't have to tell me. Shit, I'm always right. I keep telling you that."

"Girl, you are a mess. You mean that you think you're always right. Cause you're definitely not always right," I respond.

"The hell I ain't," Ilesha shouts as she flips her hair and rolls her neck.

"So, what are you going to do now? You do know you can't keep ordering dresses off the internet?" Rachel inquires.

"I'm going to do the only thing I can do and

that's hit some of these stores to see what they have. Time is ticking by too fast. Hell, it's been a month since I've been out the hospital and I still haven't found a dress. I'm getting married in five months, so I don't have time to waste. I've already wasted enough time as is," I explain.

"Baby, hitting the streets sounds like a great idea in theory, but you know Sage isn't going to go for that," Rachel remarks.

"His ass will be madder than a KKK member whose daughter married a black guy and got pregnant by him," Ilesha comments.

I damn near piss my pants from Ilesha's joke. Rachel is crying real tears from Ilesha's wise crack. That girl is nothing short of crazy. Unfortunately, she is right because Sage is very adamant about me staying in the house unless it's absolutely necessary that I leave. I'm sure he won't consider it a necessity to go out looking for a dress. Not only do I need to find a dress, I need to find a venue to have the wedding at too. I have no choice other than to go outside to get things situated. I can't bring the venues and dresses to me.

"I know girls, but he'll just have to understand that I'm fine and the only way to get this wedding done is to get out there and get it done. Besides, he didn't hire Devon to be my bodyguard only to sit in the house and listen to me playing with the boys. Oh I forgot, or to bring me some food on his way over," I narrate.

"Yeah girl, can't argue with that. You can't plan a wedding sitting in the damn house. You damn sure ain't gonna have my ass at a tired ass wedding. Hell no! I'm way to fine for that shit," Ilesha shares.

"You'll just have to explain to him as eloquently and convincingly as possible that you have to do this. I mean Sage is pretty reasonable and he'll get it. The truth is that you really can't plan the wedding from within the confines of a house. Besides, by not having access to everything you'll need to have a beautiful wedding, you'll miss out on the memorable experiences of planning a wedding," Rachel orates.

"Child, I know that's right. I have already made my decision. If Sage isn't in support of me leaving the house to plan my wedding, he'll have to be mad or just marry somebody else. I'll tell him later when he gets home," I say.

"That's my girl right there. You got a big ass backbone. Let him know that can't no man control you!" Ilesha states.

"I don't know about giving Sage an ultimatum. He doesn't seem as easily manipulated as Kevin and Eric were. God rest their souls," Rachel mentions.

"I hear you girl, but this isn't about manipulation. This is about me doing it regardless of what he says. I'm my own woman and I make my own decisions. Hell, if the guy who tried to kill me is still out there, he will always be out there. I can't stay in the house for the rest of my life," I word.

"You're so right my sister. You have to live your life because you only get one shot at it. I just want you to be safe. I don't want you to get hurt again," Rachel voices.

"Thank you, honey. Trust me, I don't want to get hurt again either, but I still have to live my life. I refuse to live in fear and confined to a house 24-7," I reply.

"I'm all for you living your life, but that's for you and your man to work out. Hell, we have my situation to work out," Ilesha remarks.

Rachel surprisingly inquires, "Do we girl? What's your situation? Are you and your man having problems?"

"Oh no honey, we are fine. My situation is that my drink is gone and Sheena hasn't replaced it yet. I mean really this is some bullshit," Ilesha answers.

I say, "Girl, you are mess. All you had to do was ask."

I get up to start making my way to get her another drink. I know she's a low-key alcoholic and I should have had another round coming. Why would I think that Ilesha was only going to have one drink especially when she has no pressing business for the rest of the day? Clearly, I'm tripping.

"I just did. And you know damn well one

drink ain't gonna do a thing for me. I'm trying to get a nice buzz before I leave," Ilesha utters.

"She's right Sheena. One isn't enough, so fix me one too while you're in there. You know what I want," Rachel adds.

"Umm, this isn't Cheers and I'm definitely not Sam Malone, so I don't get why I have to play bartender. I'm the one who was recently hospitalized, so technically you two should be catering to me," I comment.

"Bitch please. Ain't shit wrong with you. I bet you don't tell Sage that you are still recovering when he wants to fuck," Ilesha states.

"Sheena, she has you on that one. I know you give up the cookie when he asks. Bring me a bottle of water, honey. Thanks," Rachel mentions.

They're ganging up on me, so I fix the drinks without any more conversation. Besides, they're one hundred percent right. I fucked Sage as soon as I was released from the hospital. We both had needs that had to be met, so we got it in. I bring back their drinks and serve them as if I'm a cocktail waitress. They could at least tip me for affording them such great service, but that's not going to happen.

My girls and I converse while we drink. We plan out the details of my upcoming wedding such as color schemes, people in the bridal party, and ideas for the save the dates. Ilesha brings up some very kinky ideas for the bachelorette party.

We are knee deep into her suggestions and I'm super excited about them, but then we are interrupted. Unfortunately, Sage comes home and all of our girl talk comes to a screeching halt.

"My sisters, it was good while it lasted," Rachel says.

"Yessss, it has been great! And this buzz I got right now, is life," Ilesha voices.

"Yeah, I know it's been lovely. I love you ladies," I reply.

"Love you too honey. Let me get my ass home. I haven't done a damn thing I needed to do today. Over here with you and Rachel like I have a personal assistant or something," verbalizes Ilesha.

"I'll let you and Sage discuss what you need to. I need to go too. I have to prepare a presentation for work anyway. I will talk to you two later," Rachel speaks.

Rachel and Ilesha give the boys smooches, greet Sage, and depart. Sage calls me into the kitchen. When I make it to the kitchen, I see a huge bouquet of flowers. What a beautiful surprise! He's bought me an arrangement that I've never seen before. It's a combination of red roses and irises. You'd think these two flowers were meant to be placed together.

I say as I hug him, "The arrangement is absolutely breath taking. Thank you so much!"

"You're welcome. I'm glad you like them. I thought the combination was a stretch, but I think it works. The florist did her thing with them," Sage offers.

"Yessss, the florist people did their thing for real! You need to tell me which florist you got them from, so I can go there and see if they can do the flowers for the wedding," I say.

I'm glad Sage bought me these flowers because I was wondering how I was going to bring up me getting out of the house. I didn't have to think of an unnatural way to bring up the subject. Now, the conversation can happen without it being premeditated and awkward. I'm just going to tell him what it is and that's it.

"You said for you to go to?" Sage asks.

I answer, "Yes, I sure did. I know what you're going to say, but you can save it because I'm not hearing you on that. Sage, I'm trying to plan a wedding and you have to understand…"

"Sheena, wait a minute," Sage interrupts.

"No, let me finish. I need to say this. I'm trying to plan a wedding and you have to understand that I cannot and will not do this from inside this house. The internet just won't cut it, so I'm gonna be physically going to the vendors to get what we need for the wedding," I explain.

Sage, to my surprise, doesn't say anything. He just stands before me with his arms crossed as if he's calculating one of life's great mysteries. There's dead silence in the room and he's eyeballing me, so I decide to stare intently back at him. This is silly! Why is he staring at me? Finally, he speaks.

"Are you done now? Are you done telling me what you're going to do and not do?" he inquires.

"Yes, I'm done. I had to get that off of my chest before you tried to convince me otherwise. I'm serious Sage. I can't give in on this one," I answer. "You know I'm not going to let anyone mess up my wedding."

Sage verbalizes, "You could have saved that long speech if you would have let me say what I had to say. Before I was so rudely interrupted, I was gonna say that I understand that you need to get out and get the wedding plans rolling."

"Oh, so why'd you repeat back to me what I said?" I ask.

"Because you said 'you' were going to the florist, but I was thinking more like me and you can go to the florist or you and Monster can go. The way you worded it was as if you were going solo," Sage answers.

"My bad baby. I didn't know. I thought you were going to argue me down about it. Thanks for understanding my position," I voice.

"It's cool Miss. I love you no matter what. Nah, there's no need for us to fuss. Like I said, I get it," Sage mentions.

Well, that was easy. I really didn't feel like having a verbal altercation, but I would have if that's what it would have taken to get my way.

CHAPTER 7
Sheena's Perspective

Since Sage is on board with me going out to get things prepared for the wedding, I figure we should get out and about today. Time is not sitting still for anyone. There's so much to do with planning my wedding. There's so much to do that I've even considered eloping for a brief moment. However, I told myself that I won't be discouraged because the task is so cumbersome and I will give myself the wedding I've always envisioned.

"Sage, I wanna go to a few stores today, so I'm gonna get the boys ready for an outing," I say.

"That's cool. I'm ready now, so just let me know when you finish with the boys. I'll be in my office putting some things together for the lounge," Sage tells.

"K, I will. Speaking of the lounge, Ilesha took

pictures of it and sent them to me. It looks really good. They're moving with a full head of steam!" I comment.

Sage replies, "Yeah, they are. I can honestly say that they're doing their thing with it. I was going to wait a little longer before I showed you the pictures to surprise you."

"Sorry Babes, Ilesha spoiled your surprise. Hell, it looks like they're done with it," I remark.

"I know right. She sure did, but it's cool though. Well, they're done with the outside. The only thing left to do is the inside and bring in the appliances and furniture," Sage speaks excitedly.

"Oh my goodness! Already? They aren't playing any games. I wanna go see it today," I voice.

"Yes, already and no, you aren't seeing it today. Your girl already ruined some of the surprise, so I'm gonna leave something that you haven't seen to surprise you with," Sage states.

"Alright, but the not knowing is going to kill me. You just make sure I see it before anyone else," I order.

"Yes, ma'am. I will follow your orders to the letter," Sage says as he stands at attention with his hand at his brow like he's a soldier saluting.

I walk off to get the boys straight and Sage heads to his office. Both of these boys need to be changed. They must bc twins because they both have blowouts at the same time. I was hoping to make this a quick exit, but clearly my boys have other plans. What I should do is call Sage to come in here and let him change one of them too.

I'll leave him to his business and get the boys cleaned up myself. Thirty-five minutes later, I have them cleaned, changed, and ready to roll. We walk downstairs to Sage's office and I knock on his office door and I inform him that we're ready to leave. Sage swiftly pops up and we exit the house. I'm tickled that we are making moves as a family and I'll be even more elated once we are unified as one in marriage.

"Which car do you want to drive?" I inquire.

Sage answers, "We'll drive mine."

We jump into Sage's car and head to the florist first. We walk into the florist and the attendant greets us and then asks Sage if everything's alright. She thinks he's back to complain about the flowers he just picked up for me. I understand because it had to be unsettling to see him right back in here. I've worked in customer service long enough to know that when customers or clients return quickly, it's normally not for good reason.

Sage lets her know that everything is fine and that I have some questions for her. From that point, the lady and I converse about what I'm looking for and when. They have a million options to choose from and I don't know what I want to pick. I ask Sage for some help, but he's too busy playing with the boys to be any help to me. Besides that, he doesn't care about flowers anyway. Damn, I should have come with my girls.

What was I thinking trying to flower shop with a man? Well, I need to get the ball rolling, so I make a decision without my girls. Fortunately, I'm happy because my choice is beautiful. We exit the flower shop and Sage is happy that I didn't take too long deciding what I wanted.

"We got in there just about an hour ago. I would have bet money that you were gonna have us in there for at least two hours," Sage words.

"Hell, I surprised myself too! You know I can be indecisive at times," I utter.

"Tell me about it!" Sage responds assertively.

"Don't try to play me. Oh, and please don't act like you are super quick to decide on things because we both know you're not," I shoot back.

We exit the florist and walk toward the car. Sage jokes about how women are extremely froufrou and really like to waste money on things that die pretty much as soon as we buy them. I don't pay him too much mind. However, I do let him know that I've never bought flowers for myself and that it's always been a man who purchases them for me. Basically, he's talking about himself wasting money on flowers and not me. He doesn't entertain the great point I just made and is seemingly not paying me any attention. He totally catches me off guard with his next statement.

"There goes that mother fucker right there! I got his ass now!" Sage shouts.

Before I can even process what's going on, Sage darts across the parking lot of the flower shop towards his car. Now, I see what has him so interested. There's a tall black man standing by Sage's car with the door open. He's peering into the car and looks very suspicious. Finally, the guy disappears out of my line of sight and seems to be bent over inside the car. We caught the guy who's trying to kill me in the act. He's clearly trying to plant something in the car, but Sage foiled his plan. Was he planting a bomb? I don't know what the hell he's doing.

Sage makes it over to the car while the guy is still stooped over inside the car. Fortunately, Sage is in stealth mode and makes it over to the car undetected. As Sage creeps up from behind, the guy is coming up from being stooped in the car. To my horror, he's emerging from the car with a gun in his hand. Oh my goodness, Sage is about to get shot! He can't get shot right after me. What will my boys do without him if he dies?

"Sage, he has a gun!" I alert him in a frantic scream.

Sage doesn't even give the guy a chance to fully turn around when he punches the guy right in the jaw. The man's gun falls to the ground slightly under the car. The guy is wedged between Sage and the car's door and can't duck or run. I can tell the blow stuns him because he wobbles a little. He's a bit taller and thicker than Sage, so I hope Sage takes him down quickly. Sage may have met his match because the guy didn't fall like Kevin did when Sage hit him when they fought at the lounge.

The unknown man uses the car as leverage to push off of. When he pushes himself off of Sage's car, he propels himself at Sage and they go crashing into the car beside them. Fortunately, Sage is able to turn their bodies in what seems like mid-air and flings the guy into the other car back first. The window of the back-passenger door shatters from the impact. The crash is loud and violent. The thud of the impact is so loud that a lady in the flower shop steps to the door to investigate. She immediately calls 911.

Sage and this man are engulfed in full-fledged mortal combat. It seems like they're trying to kill each other. I don't know about the other guy's intentions, but I know Sage will kill him if he has to. Sage has already proven that he'll do anything to protect me, himself, and the boys. I try not to scream because I don't want the boys to get too rattled, but the fear, excitement, and anxiety overtake me.

"Babe, kick his ass! Get him babe!" I chant from a distance.

Even though I didn't want it to happen, the boys are shaken from my exaltations. They join in on the pandemonium and start crying uncontrollably. I don't know what to do to stop them from crying because I'm an emotional wreck myself. I want to take them inside, but I can't leave Sage hanging just in case he needs me. Sage and the guy are punching, scratching, and kicking one another. I hope he doesn't mess up Sage's face because I'll be mad as hell and then that guy will have to answer to me.

The guy is able to push Sage off of him as they brawl up against the car. Sage steps from between the cars and reaches down to grab the gun in his ankle strap. Now, is when the story ends. Sage is going to shoot this man and it's going to be all over. I hope he doesn't lunge for Sage because he'll be shot several times for sure. Why does Sage look so puzzled? He pats his ankle swiftly and then pats the other one. Instantaneously, he pats his waist. He's patting himself down frantically the way people do when they know they had something of importance in their pockets, but can't find it. Damn, Sage's gun must have fallen during the scuffle just as the other dude's did.

I bend down to see if I can see it from my vantage point. Although I'm looking with a hawk's eye, I can't spot his firearm. Sage quickly glances over at me and the boys and winks his eye. Sage throws his dukes up like he's a boxer in a championship bout. The guy is enraged and proceeds in the combat. The guy jabs at Sage, but he misses. Sage counters with a punch of his own, but doesn't hit the guy. The guy's arms are much longer than Sage's, so the guy has a clear advantage. My baby is going to have to get closer if he wants to land a blow.

The boxing starts to speed up as the strange man keeps approaching. He lands a clean shot on Sage's nose. Sage is hurt and stumbles back. The man knows this is his opportunity to knock Sage out, so he rushes in. The man comes in and rushes with a flurry of punches. Sage back peddles as the guy comes toward him. He has Sage on the run. I never thought I'd see the day when somebody had Sage running. To my delight, Sage lands a swift kick to the side of the guy's knee. The fellow immediately lets out a deafening scream, leans down to the side in agonizing pain, and grabs his leg.

His guard is completely down as he massages his leg. Sage doesn't give the guy a second to regain his composure. Instead, Sage punches the guy clear in his jaw with seemingly all of his might. There is a loud crack as Sage hits him and the guy falls to the pavement in a daze. Sage gives the guy three horse kicks to his midsection and the guy curls up in a ball to cover up. The fight is over and just in time. The police are pulling into the parking lot now. The officers jump out of their cars and one approaches Sage while the other approaches the guy on the ground. The police officer can easily indicate that Sage is one of the combatants. He asks for Sage's identification.

"We have reports that you were engaged in a physical altercation with that guy over there. Please, don't lie. We have your description from the 911 caller, so we know you were involved," the officer states.

"I have no reason to lie. That guy is trying to kill my fiancé and I caught his ass in the act, so I had to attack him," Sage answers. "He's lucky I didn't shoot him."

"Do you have a firearm on you sir?" the officer asks urgently.

Sage tells him that he does have a firearm, but it fell during the scuffle. Sage goes to take a step toward the direction of the pistol, but the officer immediately prevents him from doing so. The cop wants to know where the gun is and Sage tells him. The cop orders Sage to stay back while he retrieves the firearm. Sage complies and I also inform the cop that the other guy had a gun too.

The cop goes to look for the guns under the cars. He bends down under the cars and then pops back up with two items. The other officer has gotten a statement from the man who Sage beat up, so the two cops compare stories. Moments later, the cop who initially questioned us walks back over to us.

"Mr. McMillan, do you have a permit for your firearm?" he inquires.

"I sure do. It's right here in my wallet," Sage answers.

Sage gives the cop his permit and we converse. We give the officer the complete rundown of what happened from the time we exited the store. The officer tells us that our story matches the other guy's story minus a few details. Of course, the guy claims that he isn't, wasn't, and has never been trying to kill us. Additionally, the man asserts that he's never seen us before in his life and that he didn't have a gun. The cop did find Sage's gun on the ground by the battle ground, but didn't find another gun. He only found a cell phone belonging to the other guy.

I'm at such a loss for words right now. I know these cops aren't going to let this guy get away with this crap. He was clearly doing the wrong thing, but is going to make it look like Sage was the aggressor. We are not having it because we know what we saw. The guy was inside of our car.

I ask, "How does he explain being in our car? Is he denying that too?"

"No ma'am, he isn't denying that he was in your car and he admits he made a foolish decision. According to the gentleman, your car door was ajar. He said that there was a blue toy keeping the door from closing, so he came to investigate. He claims he only bothered your vehicle because he feared that there may be kids in a hot car who were trying to get out," the officer reports.

Sage speaks, "You're kidding me, right? Are

you really gonna fall for his cockamamie story?"

"The story checks out. There is no other gun anywhere, you said yourself he didn't leave the scene once the fight started, so he couldn't hide the gun, and you both stated that the fight ensued as soon as he was getting up from your backseat," the officer answers.

"Officer, it looked like he was climbing over the seats as I was approaching. He didn't have to do all of that to check to see if there were kids in the car," Sage speaks.

I chime in, "Yes, a quick glance would have been enough."

The cop further defends the man's story, "Well, he did admit that he was drawn to the car from how fancy it is. He'd never seen a Bentley SUV before, so when he saw the door ajar, he really wanted to look inside. The poor fella even took pictures of it and posted them to his Instagram account. We've verified that as well. In one post, he commented about how you have two car seats in a Bentley. I can show you the pictures if you'd like to see them."

We are beyond floored over this situation. We can't believe so much drama came out of something so minuscule. The officer informs us that Sage can file charges against the guy for trespassing and assault because he was in violation of the law for what he did. Sage doesn't want to press charges, but he does inspect his car first to make sure there are no damages to it.

Once he verifies that his car isn't damaged, we load the boys up and head back home.

Sage's hands are swollen from the fight, so I drive. We talk about how crazy today's occurrence was. I even have to come clean about something.

"Babe, I ain't even gonna lie, I thought he had you when he was swinging at your face and you were back peddling," I voice.

"That's funny! I'm surprised you thought that, but I'm glad he did. I had him right where I wanted him. That's why I winked at you," Sage says. "I thought you knew I had him at that point."

"Oh, I was wondering why you did that, but he was a lot bigger than you and his arms were longer and that's not normally good in a fight," I state.

"I feel you. It's certainly not a desirous position. That's why I had to use a little trickery to draw him in. He fell for the trap I set for him. I knew I had to take his leg out to win the fight, so I did just that," Sage explains.

We make it back to the house without incident. I settle the boys in and then tend to my man. His hands are bloody and swollen, so I wash them and rub ice on them. Next, I suck his dick until he explodes in my mouth. After that, we retire for the night cuddling in bed.

CHAPTER 8
Sheena's Perspective

"Girl, I kid you not. After all that fighting, screaming, and panic, it turned out that the guy really was just admiring Sage's car. I'm saying a person has to be a real cornball to do something like that," I inform.

Ilesha speaks, "Sheena, that's crazy as hell! These men will walk to the end of the earth to perpetrate like they have a bunch of money and drive nice cars. I mean it's really outta hand. You would think that all the fronting has to stop at some point."

I tell, "He was fronting hard too, girl. The cop showed us the photos he uploaded to Instagram from inside the car. I mean they were ridiculous! He even had a video with him talking about moving on up like George and Weezy Jefferson."

"Well, you know men think they have to prove

themselves to women with money, cars, and other trinkets, but they couldn't be more wrong. All we need is for them to be driven, loyal, attentive, and be men of their words," Rachel explains.

"Girl, yesss!" I exclaim.

"Instead of accepting his own situation, he decided to front like he has a Bentley. All it got him was his ass beat," Ilesha voices.

"He isn't the first guy to get his ass beat for fronting and he damn sure won't be the last," I interject.

"Unfortunately, you're right. They'll never change who they are because it's who they are. The days of being a proud man with integrity and morals are seemingly over. I'm blessed that I'm not still on the dating scene because it's scary out there," Rachel orates.

"Girl, I couldn't agree with you more! Men, nowadays think all they have to do is buy you dinner and then they can fuck you. I ain't bout dat life at all. I got my man and they can have the dating scene," Ilesha mentions.

"Girl, I know that's right! I feel the same way. Sage's dick was my first and I'm planning on it being my last. I am not doing the dating scene again. I can't… I can't," I state.

We chat more about the incident with Sage and the guy he fought and we also plan our course of attack on these stores today. We're going shopping for wedding items. Sage gave me his black card and told me to get whatever my heart desires. He must not know that my heart is desirous of more than he can afford, but I'll take it easy on his pockets. I have never been one to take advantage of a person who has good intent, but if I deem for a second that you are angling things selfishly in your own direction, I will burn you every time.

"What time is Devon coming over, so he can provide his bodyguard duties while we're out shopping today?" Ilesha asks.

"Devon should be here shortly, but I really don't want him to go with us. It's crazy that our girl time will be impacted tremendously because of his presence. I mean he's cool and all, but we can't bash men and be free to discuss what we want with him over our shoulders," I explain.

"That is very true. We'll just have to keep our conversation very basic. We'll just talk about work, current events, and things of that nature," Rachel suggests.

Ilesha objects, "The hell with that! I don't wanna spend my Saturday solely talking about work and current events. I have a new sex toy and a couple new positions I gotta tell you about and that's not gonna happen with Devon with us."

"That would be in poor taste to discuss things of a sexual nature with Devon in the car. I know I'd feel awkward having that discussion with him listening. We'll just save that topic for another time," Rachel says.

"Sorry, I know this entire fiasco has put an unusual strain on our girl's time. I hate that it's this way. I didn't want you ladies-my sisters to be impacted by my drama again," I mention.

"Sister, this is not your fault. We know that it's necessary and we support you when you are up and down. That's the way it's been and that's the way things will always remain," Rachel orates.

Ilesha states, "Hell, we'll just work around him and improvise. You know how we do it. We always make it happen."

I know it's not an extremely big deal to Rachel and Ilesha that Devon will be tagging along with us, but I know it's at least slightly bothersome to them. It only makes sense that they would be faintly bothered by his attendance because the entire dynamic of our time together will be altered. None of us can truly discuss what we want or act how we want because Devon might tell our business. The last thing any of us want is for our business to be in the streets. We've never been the types of females to have our business on blast.

We even curved dudes growing up because they used to talk too much. We were so discreet that we wouldn't talk to dudes from Linden High because we knew they'd have our business in the hallways at school. I remember the time when Ilesha slapped a dude square across the face in the second-floor tunnel. The guy she slapped was going around the school telling everybody that she gave him head, but she really hadn't. When Ilesha got word about what he said she came and got Rachel and me immediately.

We rolled up on the guy while he was politicking in the second-floor tunnel and without a word, Ilesha slapped him so hard that her palm print was imbedded in the dude's face. The slap was so loud that people said they heard it upstairs. Mad people were in the tunnel when she slapped him and that event became known as "the slap heard around the school". The guy was so stunned that he didn't even attempt to hit her back. I was glad he didn't because we would have had to jump him. We've always felt like a woman's most intimate secrets and doings should be kept as quiet as possible and lying about it is even worse. We don't get how women today put all of their business out for everyone to see, but to each his own.

I really want to be able to chat with my girls openly and freely today. I really feel like we need to be able to do this. Today is the perfect day for us to do it. The sun is out and the temperature is great! I'm free as a bird because the boys are with Sage today. Sage and the boys left early this morning to go meet his mom in Alexandria, Virginia for the weekend.

I have no kids or a man to tend to and I can't even chill with my girls the way I want. The hell with it! Me and my girls are going to have our day and we're going to have it the way we want it to be! There's nothing else to talk about.

"Hey, I'm thinking that we don't have to wait for Devon to get here for us to go. There's strength in numbers and there's three of us and it's broad daylight, so we'll be fine without my bodyguard," I bring up.

"Sheena, I don't know about that. Besides, you and Sage have an agreement that you'll use Devon's bodyguard services," Rachel responds.

I say, "I know what I said and I will use his services, but I'm just gonna give us a few hours of girl time and then I'll call Devon and tell him I need him."

"You're a grown ass woman and what you agreed on with your man is between you and him. Hell, if you say you'll be fine then I trust what you say. Just let me know, but I know one thing and that's that my ass ain't driving," Ilesha blurts out.

"Well, it is daytime and we'll be in public locations, so I guess it'll be fine. I just hope if Sage finds out, he doesn't think we swayed you to disregard the pact you two had," Rachel vocalizes.

"Umm, Sage know damn well he better not bother me with some mess about why I let Sheena leave the house. Hell, I'll curse his ass out for bothering me," Ilesha remarks.

"He won't blame you two for anything. Nobody is cursing anybody out and Sage or Devon won't even know what we did," I reply.

"Here Sheena goes again. Damn, girl…you know you are always scheming and I love it! Tell us what you have in mind," Ilesha says.

"Yes, you are. I don't know if I even want to know what you're cooking up," Rachel comments.

"I'm not that bad, so don't do me like that. Y'all just tried my life. I only scheme when I have to. And let's be for real here, I'm just telling a little white lie to protect Sage's feelings," I explain.

"I hear you girl! That doesn't necessarily mean that I believe it though," Ilesha says jokingly.

"Well, I'm telling y'all anyway. Here's what I'm going to do. I'm going to tell Devon that I'm not gonna hit the streets until later today and that he doesn't need to come over to escort me until later. During the time he thinks I'm home, I'll really be out and about with my favorite ladies. By the time the few hours go by, we'll be done doing us and already be back home. Then I'll tell Devon to come over because I need to go to the grocery store and let him carry the bags for me," I detail.

"That's so deceitful of you Sheena, but I can't tell you what to do. I'll support you whichever way you choose to proceed," Rachel says.

"Hell, you know I don't care about what you tell your man. Let's get outta here then! I'm ready to be seen in this tight ass sundress. I know my ass is all over the place," Ilesha remarks.

I call Devon and tell him to pause on coming over to escort me. I also inform him that he can come by the house at 4pm. Devon agrees to come over at the time I requested. Now, I'm free to hang with my girls without any impediments. We can speak freely and hang the way we like to hang. In a blink of an eye, we are out the door and heading to get out eyebrows done. After we get our eyebrows done, we head over to Bridal's Boutique.

Bridal's Boutique is a store inside the mall that specializes in custom made dresses for brides. They have the most exquisite dresses. I was in a wedding a few years ago and the bride purchased a dress from them and it was absolutely breathtaking. Ever since then, I had Bridal's Boutique on my radar for a place to get my dress. I would have visited them a while back to see about my dress if Sage wasn't so paranoid. What I really like about them is that every dress is custom made and they can do it in record time. I consider myself to be a cut above the rest, so I don't want to be in a dress that someone else may be seen in. They are pricey, but you have to be willing to pay for top quality merchandise and expeditious service.

We park the car and head inside. We are greeted warmly and promptly by their staff. They ask us who's the bride-to-be and I step to the forefront. I'm asked what style of dress I'm looking for, but I don't know. I've always wanted to be married, but I never imagined anything other than the train. I've always felt it was very elegant and princess-like to have a long train behind me as I walk down the aisle. Other than that, I don't know what I want. The lady attending to me is very knowledgeable about dresses which helps ease my anxiety about picking something. This is likely to be the most magical moment of my life and makes me a bit nervous because I'll be devastated if everything's not perfectly carried out.

She shows me several dresses they have in the store as well as what they have in their catalog. Rachel, Ilesha, and I look through their inventory while we discuss my best option. After looking through everything they have to offer, we decide on a dress that is a viable option. The boutique is able to combine features from one dress with the features from other dresses to give me the custom design I desire. To my delight, the store's seamstress can have the dress done in two months. That's good because that gives me plenty of time to get any alterations made that might be necessary on the back end. I'd hate to cut it close and not have time to spare on the back end if I need it.

The girls and I don't depart the mall when we finish in that store. Instead, we walk around the mall and shop at other stores. This is definitely time well spent with them. I really needed to get out and have some fun. I've been nowhere other than the doctor's office and home since I was shot.

Ilesha is prancing around the mall sizing up all the females in here. As always, she's criticizing them for not being as fine as she is. She even questions their sense of style. Rachel, who's not normally one to criticize or pass judgment, even sides with Ilesha on some of the outfits and ridiculousness she's seeing.

"Oh my goodness! Look at her face. Damn, that lil girl better hope it doesn't rain," Ilesha states.

"Who's face?" Rachel inquires.

Ilesha answers, "The girl to the left with the red leggings on."

"What's wrong with her face and why does she need to hope it doesn't rain?" I ask.

"Poor child done painted her whole damn face on. Look at those eyebrows. If it rains and her face gets wet, she's gonna look like she dipped her face in tar," Ilesha jokes.

"Girl, you're a mess. Leave that lil girl alone. That's somebody's child right there. She's trying," I voice.

"Yes, she may not know any better. Bless her heart," Rachel chimes in.

"I'll leave her alone, but her mother needs to tell her. Hell, one of her lil friends should've have told her something. Letting her walk around looking crazy, like she right," Ilesha utters. "I ain't never gonna come out the house looking crazy, but if I do, one of your asses better let me know."

"Girl, now you know we don't even play like that! We have never and will never let any of us walk around looking crazy," I reply.

"No, we've never done that. That would be so unbecoming of our sisterhood. We always have to come forward with the truth even if it hurts," Rachel comments.

We've done all of the shopping that we're going to do, so it's time to leave the mall. Not to mention, I've already overstayed my time here. I wanted to make a quick run to Bridal's Boutique, but there was nothing quick about it if you add in the time we've been in the mall. My plan of a quick trip went out the window hours ago and I hope Sage doesn't start to look for me.

As we head to the car, we walk past a men's suit store and see a familiar, but not so friendly face. Marcus comes walking out of the store and nearly barrels into us. Ilesha is immediately infuriated by his, in her opinion, intentional act.

"I'm gonna need for you to watch where you're going. I mean damn, this isn't a race track that you're on," Ilesha remarks.

"I remember you ladies. The all-white party from a while back. I see all of you are still hanging tough. Sorry, about almost crashing into you. I'm in a rush to handle some business," Marcus states.

"Yeah, it's us and we're still here and I see that

you still don't have your wedding ring on your finger just like before," I say.

Ilesha states, "Still on your bullshit I see. Same conniving ass man as you were before. Doing that poor girl like that. I don't even know her, but I know she's too good for you."

"Actually, we're not together anymore thanks to that big ass scene you made that night at the all-white party. Somebody told my wife and one thing lead to another. Before I knew it, I was kicked out of the house and paying child support," Marcus explains.

"Hell, that ain't got shit to do with us! That's your fault for being trifling. Own your shit and stop trying to blame others," Ilesha voices.

"No, if your asses hadn't gone overboard and caused someone to contact my wife, I would have been fine. Now, I'm down and out and you bitches are running around town like life is sweet," Marcus states with an attitude.

Ilesha inquires as she swings and strikes him, "Bitches? Who in the hell you calling bitches? Are you out of your damn mind?"

Ilesha lands the smack clean across Marcus's face. He rubs his hand in the exact location of the smack and takes a step back. I can tell he wants to body slam Ilesha, but he refrains from doing so. Marcus is very lucky that he didn't attempt to harm her because she has her blade on her and would cut him with no problem if he tried anything physical. Rachel attempts to get us to move on and forget about Marcus. She is not one for drama and public spectacles. Rachel is our voice of reason.

"Come on ladies, we should go now. He wasn't worth our time at the all-white party and he still isn't today," Rachel states.

We decide to walk away from Marcus and head to the car. I know I don't have time for any extra altercations because I have enough going on already. Ilesha is satisfied with her slap and begins to walk away at Rachel's request. Unfortunately, Marcus isn't done with us and decides to follow us.

"Wait, you slap me for being trifling, but Sheena is just as trifling as me, if not more. Don't try to play like she's innocent because she's not. She was fucking those two dudes at the same time. Yeah, I heard about that," Marcus says.

I reply, "First of all, you need to stop following us. Secondly, you don't know anything about my situation, so get your tired ass on and stay out of my damn business."

"Typical response. You did what I did, but you want to sweep your shit under the rug and gloss over it. Well, that's not gonna happen. Bitch, you'll get yours in the end. You ruined my life and think that you don't have to suffer any consequences from it. You got the courts taking child support and alimony out of my check and now I'm struggling," Marcus complains.

"Don't blame my girl for your life amounting to nothing. You shoulda been loyal to your woman and you wouldn't be in your situation. Your lady needed to know about you and I can speak for all of us and say that we're glad she found out, but we didn't tell her. We didn't think about you after that night," Ilesha orates.

"Hell, we didn't think about you after that moment," I throw in.

"Y'all can kiss my ass! This shit ain't over. Hell no, it's not over," Marcus warns.

We don't give Marcus another moment of our time. We see a security guard in the mall as Marcus follows us and continues to harass us. Marcus sees him too and decides to fall back from trailing us. My girls and I exit the mall and walk to my car. We jump in the car and I go to start it, but it doesn't crank. What in the world is wrong with my car? My car is only a year old and doesn't have many miles on it, so it shouldn't be giving me any problems.

I wait a minute and attempt to start the car again, but it doesn't turn over. It doesn't appear to be getting any power, so it must be the battery. I didn't leave anything on and we were only in the mall for a few hours, so I don't get how it isn't getting any power. I have to get a jump, but I don't have any jumper cables.

"I'm sorry y'all. I don't know what's wrong with this car. This has never happened before. This is crazy," I say.

Rachel responds, "Girl please. You don't have to apologize for your car breaking down. It's not your fault. Besides, you know they don't make these cars to last like they used to."

"I know that's right. It probably just needs a jump. I'll go back in the mall and find one of them security guards to see if they can give us a jump," Ilesha states.

Ilesha goes back into the mall to see if we can get a jump. Ten minutes later she returns with a security guard in his patrol vehicle. He pulls up beside my car and jumps out with his cables. I pop the hood and he attaches the cables to my battery. I try to start the car again, but again, my car doesn't turn over. I guess it's something more severe than the battery.

"Ladies, I'm sorry the jump didn't work. You may have to call someone to tow the car if you can't get it started. Let me know if there's anything else I can help you with," the security guard says.

We thank the man for his willingness to help us out. He jumps back in his vehicle and departs. Now, we have to figure out what we're going to do. It's not like Sage is around to come get us and I really don't feel like having an argument about me being out. I really just need to get the car towed to the house.

"So, what you wanna do girl? How are you gonna get your car home?" Ilesha inquires.

"You should get it towed to the shop. That's

easiest," Rachel suggests.

"I'm gonna get the car towed, but not to the shop. I'll get it towed to the house and act like it broke down there. That way Sage will never know that I was even out of the house," I say. "We can just Uber back to my place."

"Girl, you know you have a deceitful mind and I love it. Hell, that's even better for you because you know that Sage will either fix it himself or pay someone to get it back right," Ilesha remarks.

Rachel utters, "Yes, he'll never know and you'll avoid an argument for sure."

I comment confidently, "I know. Y'all know I got this. Girls, we've been through far worse situations than this. Some car trouble is child's play for us. Sage won't know and I'll call Devon over as soon as we get back to the house."

I use Rachel's phone to call the tow truck company. I use her phone because I don't want the tow truck people calling my phone back one day while I'm with Sage and then I'll have to explain myself. Ilesha summons the Uber and there's one in the area. Unfortunately, the Uber driver arrives before the tow truck does and has to wait with us. The tow truck driver arrives about twenty minutes later and puts my car on the flatbed. I give the driver the address to my house and we leave the mall. While we're riding in the Uber, my phone starts ringing.

"Damn, girls. It's Sage calling!" I exclaim.

"Damn, don't answer it. You know he'll

throw a storm at you if he knows what's up. I would let the call go straight to your voicemail," Ilesha mentions.

Rachel offers, "She's right Sheena. We'll be back to your place shortly, so you can just call him back then."

I take their advice and don't answer the call. Sage will just have to think that I'm asleep or busy doing something and missed the call. We're almost to my place, so it doesn't make sense to come clean now. Sage won't be any of the wiser if I hold out just a little longer. As soon as his incoming call ends, he calls right back. I'm tempted to answer the phone to find out what he wants, but I know he doesn't want or need anything. I decide not to take his call again.

We are a couple of blocks from the house and I start feeling better about the situation. My stomach is finally loosening up after being tight since we left the house earlier today. I was really worried about Sage finding out about me leaving the house without Devon. Hell, I could be relaxing too prematurely. What if Sage is at the house and is calling me because I'm not there. Damn, I should have just let Devon tag along with us. Oh well, I've made my bed, so I'll just have to lie in it.

We finally make it to my block and I can see the house. I don't see Sage's car in front of the house, so I know he's not home. Thank goodness for that. We would have had the Super

Bowl of arguments today. The tow truck driver begins to let the car down into the driveway. The Uber driver stops the car and gets out to open the back door for Ilesha and Rachel. He's been so nice to us the entire ride and is really working hard for an extra tip. I don't mind tipping for good service, so I reach in my wallet to give him a little extra to show my appreciation for such stellar service.

Ilesha and Rachel get out and then the driver walks to the front door to let me out. He lifts the handle, but the door doesn't immediately open. He looks confused as to why the door isn't opening and motions to me to try the handle from inside the car. I pull the door handle from inside the car, but again the door fails to open.

"I'm sorry the door is stuck. I may have the child protection lock on or something. I apologize," he states.

He walks around to the driver's side of the car and opens the door. He sits in the seat and begins hitting buttons to make the door release as I attempt to open my door. Unfortunately, his efforts are futile because the door doesn't give.

"Damn, well I guess this kills my tip," he says jokingly. "I just knew I was gonna get a good tip and a great rating from you."

"These things happen from time to time. Hell, my car stopped working out of the clear blue sky, so I'm not gonna hold it against you. You're the reason we were able to make it back here and you waited with us while the tow truck came," I reply.

I decide to climb into the driver's seat, so I can exit through that door, but the driver won't move. He's blocking me from getting out of the car and pushes me back down forcefully. When he pushes me back I hit my head on the passenger's window. I let out a scream that alerts Rachel and Ilesha, but before they have time to react, the driver closes his door and speeds off.

Ilesha runs after the car for a few steps, but then stops because we are too far ahead. Rachel is screaming for someone to do something and appears to be dialing her phone. I hope she's calling 911. I fight the driver as he drives away, but I can't get the upper hand. I hope to make him crash or at least slow down, but it's not working. I slap and punch at him, but none of the blows faze him. His arms are a lot longer than mine are and I can't get past his outstretched arm to really connect on him. The driver is swinging back at me as he steers the car with his other hand. Unfortunately, his blows faze me every time he hits me.

"Damn, you're one feisty bitch. You didn't even fight this much when I broke into your house and attacked you there. What a difference a day makes," he speaks.

"That was you at my house that night? Why are you doing this to me?" I inquire as we continue our skirmish.

"Revenge," he responds coldly.

I can't possibly imagine why he wants revenge. I don't know this guy from Joe Blow. It just doesn't make sense. I know I can't win this battle from the front seat, so I muster up all of my strength and thrust myself into the back seat. Now, I have the upper hand. I get behind the driver and start punching him in the back of the head. He tries to fend me off without losing control of the car.

To my dismay, he doesn't slow the car down at all. Next, I grab him around his neck and proceed to choke him. While I'm choking him, he slows the car down just as I hoped he would. I stop choking him for a split second, so I can try the door handle. Damn, the back door is locked just as the front doors are. My kidnapper speeds back up and is dipping in and out of traffic. I have to get out of this car before he makes it to his intended destination. I know the windows can't be shatter proof, so I begin kicking the window with all my might.

I kick once and the window gives, but doesn't break. I know I'm onto something, so I give the window another swift kick. The window budges again, but yields the same results as the first kick. What the hell can I do to break this window? Maybe I just need more force behind my kicks. I decide to thrust the window with both feet at the same time. One, two, three… I kick and to my delight the window shatters. I clear the broken fragments of glass and hang out the window in an attempt to get someone's attention.

"Help! Somebody, help me!" I scream at the top of my lungs.

I must have the worst luck in the world because there are no cars on the street. I see a car driving up from behind us, but who knows if they'll catch up to us. I know I have to slow the car down, so I take off my belt and wrap it around the Uber driver's neck as he speeds down the street. I have him right where I want him again. He's flailing his arms around trying to reach me, but his efforts are to no avail. I have my back pressed firmly against the back seat and I have my feet braced against his seat to give me more strength to choke him.

My tactics are not in vein because he's fighting less and begins to slow the car down again. I know he's about to pass out, so I keep the pressure going full throttle. Once the car slows down to a decent speed I'm jumping out of the window. I'll just have to take my chances with a few bumps and bruises. I have his ass now! My confidence is high and I can taste freedom. The car is doing thirty-five miles per hour at the most and I'm almost ready to make my move.

Just as I'm preparing to make my move, the driver slams on the brakes. He catches me off guard and then he yanks the lever on the side of his seat that allows the seat to go forward and backward. He plants his feet into the floor of the car and with all his might, he swiftly pushes the seat back. Unfortunately, that stunt gives him an inch or two of space between his neck and the belt. He's able to grip the belt and end the choking. I sense the tables are turning, so I drop the belt and try to climb out the window. The car I saw when I initially broke the window is almost to us and I'm hoping it's a good Samaritan who will be willing to help me.

I attempt to make the move out of the window and I'm stunned in my tracks. I feel like I'm being electrocuted. I hear a sound that I've only heard in police videos and I feel two hooks in my skin. I'm sure that's the sound of a Taser and from the way I feel, I know I'm being zapped with one. My body is as stiff and unforgiving as a steel beam. I am stopped in my tracks and have no control of my motor skills. I can't do anything to help myself out of this conundrum, but I'm completely cognizant of everything that's going on.

The driver has me right where he wants me and that's defenseless. Next thing I know, he's speeding away again. Hell, all that work I did was for nothing. I tasted freedom only to have it yanked away from me. I guess this is why Sage wanted me to stay in the house or take Devon with me. I know my girls have given the police a description of this car by now, so hopefully they'll be able to find me before this creep gets his revenge.

Every time I gain some composure this guy

shocks me with the stun gun. I'm becoming slightly disoriented and everything is moving in slow motion. I feel as if I'm going to pass out. He turns a few more corners and then he pulls in a parking garage on Maryland Ave. I caught a glimpse of the sign as we turned the corner. I hope I can use this information to help me at some point.

He says, "Sheena, time to switch out of this car. I know every cop in the district is looking for this car by now. Trust me, I've thought of everything. You know I'm glad I didn't kill you at your house. I want you and your people to suffer the way I do every day and believe me, you're going to suffer. They say payback's a bitch!"

Damn, just as I was thinking that the police would surely see the car driving down the street, he pulls into a parking garage where nobody will be looking for us. Furthermore, he's going to switch the cars out.

"Sir, I don't know you, but whatever I've done to you, I am truly sorry and apologize immensely and sincerely. Just let me go and I can make it up to you," I plead.

"No, bitch! There's nothing you or anybody can do to prevent what's going to happen to you. You're gonna be begging me to kill you quickly. Watch and see," he orates.

The thought of my current predicament and his sinister remarks send a frightening chill throughout my body. Reality is setting in and I understand that I may not see my boys again. I try to reach for the plugs of the Taser to take them out, but my assailant presses the trigger and shocks me again. My body goes limp to the point where I'm very weak. I have no strength to do anything. My kidnapper pulls into a parking spot and jumps out of the car urgently. He opens the door of the car beside us, opens the back door of the car where I'm resting, snatches me up, and throws me in the back seat of the car he pulled up beside. He ties my hands and feet with a rope and closes the door. The Uber driver calmly gets in the driver seat of the car he switched us into and backs out of the space. Now, nobody will be able to track us down. The only thing the police or anyone could use to find me is now abandoned in this parking garage. I can't even fight back anymore to help my cause.

CHAPTER 9
Sage's Perspective

Why is Sheena's car on a flatbed truck? Furthermore, why are they in that car? Oh, she must have had car trouble while she was sneaking out with her girls. I can't believe she really pulled the fifty-two fake out on Monster and told him she was staying home today. I know she's going to be extremely surprised when I pull up on her. I bet she didn't answer my call because she didn't want me to know that she in fact did leave the house. She betrays my trust and goes against her word for what? I don't get it. All I'm trying to do is keep her safe while the police try to find her attacker. I know she's quite skilled in the art of deception, but there's no way she'll be able to wiggle out of this one. However, I'm sure she'll try to make it something that it's not.

I hate that I got caught at this traffic light. I

want to pull up on her while she and her friends are still in the car, so she can't deny anything. If she doesn't know that I actually saw her in the car, she'll never admit it. She comes from the school of thought that says if they didn't put their hands on you, it wasn't you. Come on light…change for goodness sakes. I don't think this light has ever been this long and I get stopped by this light frequently. Finally, the light changes and I proceed to my house to hopefully catch Sheena, my love, red-handed.

I make it to my house just in time to see the tow truck backing into the driveway to drop her car. Unfortunately, he has the road blocked as he's doing so and I can't get around him. What I do enjoy is that his truck is obstructing anyone's view of me waiting on the other side of this truck. I want to jump out of my car right now and run over to her, but I'd have to leave my car in the street, since there's nowhere to park on my block. It's okay, I'll wait because I've already seen enough to refute any claims that she may make about how she ended up getting her car towed. She probably would have told me that either Rachel or Ilesha borrowed her car and then had car trouble, so she told her to get it towed back here. I'm not hearing any of that.

Well, how long does it take to back a truck into a driveway? This guy must be a rookie or something. He must not have the wheel as many people who drive trucks claim they do. I grow frustrated from watching the driver go back and forth, so I jump out and begin to walk around the truck. As I clear the truck, I see Ilesha and Rachel standing on my porch looking back at the street with a look of concern on their faces. I wonder where Sheena is until I look over at the car that all three of them were in. My stomach plummets to my feet faster than an elevator with no brakes and snapped cables can fall to the bottom floor. I look through the car's rear windshield and see my fiancé slumped in the passenger's seat.

I take off towards Sheena faster than Allyson Felix runs to win the Gold Medal, but the driver closes the door only after I take two steps. Without a second's hesitation, I turn around to get in my car. Unfortunately, the tow truck driver is still attempting to back into the driveway and is currently blocking the street. He has to get out of the way!

I scream, "Just back the damn truck all the way into the driveway! Somebody's has kidnapped my fiancé and I need to get through!"

The driver follows my orders, but is still blocking the street to a certain degree. I'm back in my vehicle and I know I have no choice, but to get through, so I punch the gas and squeeze through the small amount of space that's left in the street for me to pass. There's a violent scraping noise as I pass by. I know my car is badly damaged, but I don't care. I see the tow truck driver throwing his hands up in objection to me having destroyed the front of his truck.

I get through the road block and I can see what looks to be the car that Sheena is in far ahead. To my anger, traffic is not flowing as speedily as I need it to, so I have to dip and dodge in and out of traffic. Unfortunately, I'm not making up the ground that I need to. I have to keep up with this car. While I'm driving, I call 911 and give them a description of the car that Sheena's in and inform them of what I'm doing. The 911 dispatch lets me know that the cops have been called, but wants me to stop my pursuit of them. I end the call and continue chasing them down.

I'm still caught up in the traffic and it seems that I will stay that way if I don't do something now. I can ram this car in front of me out of the way and then I'll be free to accelerate as much as I need to catch up to them. Damn, I can't do that. I'll be a sitting duck if I cause severe damage to my car and it stops working. I pound the steering wheel in frustration. Drastic times call for drastic measures. I insanely dip out of my lane and drive head on into oncoming traffic, so I can get around. It's a risky move, but it's my only option. Fortunately, I can still see the car Sheena's in up ahead. They must have stopped or slowed down a bit because they should be further along than they are.

I'm not complaining and will accept any

blessing that is sent my way or Sheena's. Unfortunately, cars are now coming toward me, so I dip back into my proper lane and barely avoid a head-on collision. The kidnapper's car speeds up, but I'm gaining ground on them. I just hope he doesn't turn off this street and I lose them. For that reason, I opt to reduce my speed, so not to alert the driver of my presence and cause him to deviate from his route. Just as I'm slowing down, their car turns off of the street and out of my line of sight. I have no option other than to gun it, so I do just that.

I zoom up to 16th Street and turn so fast that I almost flip my car over in the process. I turn the corner and I am at a loss. There isn't a trace of the car, the driver, or of Sheena. Fuck! Where the hell did they go? I have a clear view straight up 16th, but I don't see them. There isn't even an immediate turn on a perpendicular street they could have taken. Damn, I lost them! I drive to the next block past the parking garage and figure the only place they could have went is in it, so I turn around and enter.

I drive through the entrance of the parking garage without taking a ticket and take down the gate arm. I drive through the garage scanning and scrutinizing everything I see. Unfortunately, I don't see anything moving or even out of place, but I keep driving and observing. I go to the next level of the garage and don't see any cars on this level at all. As I'm driving to the get to the top floor of the garage, a car is driving past me going in the opposite direction. I look over at the car, but don't see anything out of place, so I proceed past.

There is only one car on this floor and it's the one Sheena was in. I drive over to it and immediately see that the car is abandoned. Sheena has to be in the car that just drove past me, so I turn around and speed through the parking garage like I'm Superman on a mission to save Lois Lane. This time I'm not taking the chance of driving slow, so he won't know I'm coming. I'm glad that he doesn't have that much of a lead on me and he's probably still driving cautiously to not alert anyone of his movements.

My tires are screeching loudly and my adrenaline is pumping profusely. I don't know what I'm going to do if I get my hands on this guy. Should I shoot him dead or beat the life out of him? I'll figure it out when I get the opportunity. I make it down to the bottom floor and see the car I suspect to have Sheena in it paying to exit the garage. I know once that car makes it to the street that I could lose sight of it forever. I've got to stop it from exiting. I don't even know for sure that Sheena's in the car, but it's a chance I have to take.

If I don't stop this car here and now, I'll always wonder if Sheena was in there. I can't afford to carry that burden and I can't afford to take that chance with Sheena's life. Honestly, if

I'm wrong about the guy in the car and I crash into him, it'll only be a traffic accident. I'm covered; that's what I pay insurance for. I put my seatbelt on and step on the gas. I ram the car just as the arm bar for his car to exit is rising. There is a thunderous crunch as our two cars collide. I hit the back of the car and pushed it up against the cement median holding the gate arms.

Simultaneously, I hear a woman's scream. I don't know for sure if it's Sheena, but I sure am eager to find out. The man in the car is dazed for a moment and is trying to gather himself. I attempt to unlock my seatbelt, but it's jammed. Although it's stuck, I can reach my gun and knife. I start cutting the seatbelt free when I see the man has finally gained his composure. I see him turn to make a move for the back seat. I don't know what his intentions are, so I grab my gun and fire a shot at him.

As I had hoped firing the shot would do, the man ducks down and then runs out of the parking structure. I resume cutting myself out of my seatbelt and then try to open my door, but it's jammed shut, so I climb over the seat and exit through the back door. I dart to the car in hopes of seeing Sheena alive and well. When I examine the backseat of the car, I see Sheena tied up squirming on the backseat of the car.

I open the door immediately to pull her up. I take out my pocket knife and cut her free. We embrace as she cries in the protection of my arms. Sheena is visibly shaken and for good reason.

"Oh my goodness. You're the last person I wanted to see, but definitely the person I hoped to see," Sheena says as she weeps.

"I hoped to see you too. That's why I'm here now, so there's no need to worry. You can relax now. You're safe," I reply.

"The boys?" Sheena inquires.

I answer, "The boys are fine. They're with my mother in Alexandria. Don't worry about them because we need to make sure you are in good shape."

"I think I'm fine. Just was thinking it might be my last days and that I'd die without seeing you or the boys again," Sheena voices.

"You don't have to ever worry about that because we're going to grow old together. That I can promise you," I assert.

"Old and grey?" Sheena asks jokingly.

"You may get grey hairs, but I'm not. Don't try to put that on me," I speak.

Staring death in the face will shake up even the strongest person. I know when I got shot I thought I was breathing my last few breaths. I call 911 back and alert them to our location. About five minutes later, the police begin filing into the parking garage. There are twelve units present and an ambulance. The cops begin taking a statement from Sheena and me while they treat us for minor injuries.

Gladly, I'm only faintly sore from the crash and have no cuts or bruises. They examine Sheena too, but find no severe injuries to her either. Several of the units comb the area to find the driver of the car once I inform them that he fled on foot. Other officers on the scene go to retrieve evidence from the vehicle Sheena was initially abducted in. Sheena tells us exactly how she and her friends ended up in the Uber to begin with.

The cops who went to check the car that was abandoned in the parking garage find a man stuffed in the trunk of the car. Fortunately, he's going to be alright, but suffered a blow to his head that needs to be treated, so they are taking him to the hospital. It is determined that the entire situation with Sheena's car breaking down, the Uber driver showing up, and the kidnapping was just an elaborate plan by the assailant to snatch Sheena.

He clearly watched Sheena and her friends go to the mall. While they were in the mall, he found a way to disable her car. At the same time, the perpetrator called an Uber for himself and then hit the driver over the head and tossed him in the trunk. From the point when he knew he had disabled Sheena's car and had overtaken the real Uber driver, he needed a little luck that Sheena would seek a driver and he'd most likely be the closest one to her. The rest was easy for him because all he had to do was get them in the car.

The police figure he must have followed them to the mall to begin with. They even consider the possibility of an accomplice. The cops find some of Sheena's belongings in the abduction car, so they give them back to her. They decide to take the car back to their lot to check for more evidence. I wish when I shot at the guy I would have killed him then. We could have ended this fiasco today. The officers who went to search for Sheena's kidnapper inform us that he's long gone.

"Ma'am, is there anything else you can tell us? Did you notice any cars following you to the mall?" Officer Mosely asks.

Sheena answers, "No, I didn't see a thing. Maybe my girls did, but I doubt it because they would have pointed it out then. I mean everything seemed normal. They're on their way here now."

Officer Mosely states, "Okay, well if anything else comes to mind please give us a call. We really need to get to the bottom of this. I don't want to scare you, but you could be in harm's way every day this guy remains at large."

"I will if something comes to mind," Sheena responds.

"Detective Mosely, there has to be a way to track the perpetrator through the Uber app. In order for him to have ordered the Uber to begin with, he would've had to have an account," Sage verbalizes.

Detective Mosely responds, "That's absolutely right, so I'll contact the Uber company to get the records. We'll use the technology he used to get Sheena, to capture him. Great idea Sage!"

Moments later, Rachel and Ilesha arrive at the garage and they are questioned by the police. Unfortunately, they don't have anything to add that will help the investigation, so the conversation is very short. The police have all they need, so they depart. My car is totaled and is not drivable, so Sheena and I ride back to the house with Rachel and Ilesha. On the way back to the house, we converse about the happenings of the day.

"Sister, I'm so glad that you're okay. I almost died when the driver pulled off with you in the car. It was all just so surreal," Rachel speaks from the heart.

"Girl, I know that's right. It all happened so fast. One minute we were all in the car and then we looked back and you two were zooming away. I went to reach for my knife, but the car was gone before we got to take a step," Ilesha reports.

Rachel states, "The next thing I knew, Sage was crashing cars and zooming past in pursuit of you. Your king was going to rescue his queen in distress. The fact that he did just that is beautiful in itself."

Sheena verbalizes, "I guess it was pretty heroic how he came to my rescue. I really don't know where I'd be without him."

"Umm, ya ass would still be abducted. That's where you'd be," Ilesha blurts out.

"Ilesha, don't say that. That's so insensitive of you. Sheena just had a traumatic experience. Give her some compassion," Rachel advises.

"Hell, she's fine. She's here with us, so we can see that she's okay," Ilesha remarks.

"Sage, how did you manage to come to my rescue? When did you get back to town? How did you know I was in trouble?" Sheena probes mystified.

I explain, "I told Monster, well Devon, to call me once he made it to the house and all was well, but he actually texted me and told me that you cancelled. At the time, I thought nothing of it, but then a little while later I thought better of your supposed decision to stay in. Next thing I know, you are at the mall, so I sent Monster to the mall to check on you. I called you, but you didn't answer.

"Now, that doesn't make any sense Sage. You couldn't have possibly known that I was at the mall if you were in Virginia," Sheena cuts in.

"Thanks for cutting me off, but if you let me finish, I'll tell you how it all unfolded," I shoot back.

"Excuse me! Go ahead Sage. I really wanna hear this one," Sheena comments.

"Thank you for granting me permission to continue. Monster got to the mall and couldn't find you, so I left Virginia and headed back to

D.C. Now, I knew you or at least your car was at the mall because I left my iPad in your car from when the boys were playing with it. I checked the app to locate it and it read that the car was at the mall," I explain.

"I was headed to the mall when I noticed the car was moving. From the direction the car was headed, I determined that you were finally headed home, so I called again, but you didn't answer. I figured you snuck out and didn't want me to know. As the timing worked out, I was right behind the tow truck, but got caught at the light, so I was a minute or two behind you ladies pulling up and the rest is history. I saw you get taken away and pursued," I narrate.

"Well damn, we have a real live Liam Neeson over here," Ilesha vocalizes. "At least in the movie, the guy knew who the people were, but we have no idea who or why this sick fuck is doing what he's doing."

"Right, that's me. I will find you and kill you! I'm just glad something told me to head back when I did. A minute or two later and I would have missed you completely. We'll figure it out and find this guy. We have to," I reply.

We get back to the house and continue replaying the events of today as if we will tell a different story. All of the girls partake in adult beverages as I look at my security cameras of the house to see if I see anything that's out of place. I'm being nice to Sheena while her friends are here, but when they leave she'll be getting an earful about how selfishly, dishonestly, and irresponsibly she acted today.

CHAPTER 10
Sheena's Perspective

Well, Sage has chewed my ass out the last few days because I put myself in danger the other day. I know it was a bad move looking back, but how was I supposed to know that it would turn out as badly as it did. I'm glad I was blessed with a lot of ass because with all the chewing Sage did, I wouldn't have any left. I like my ass eaten sexually, but definitely not the way Sage got at me. He did the most for sure. I have too much to do today. This wedding planning is kicking my ass. Raising two boys, running a successful business, and keeping my man satisfied are no easy tasks by themselves and now I'm planning a wedding on top of it all. I must be crazy!

I know I really don't want to wait for Monster to get here, but I have no choice. I guess my impatience is a gift and a curse. It's a gift because it allows me to be independent and a curse because I don't wait for people and sometimes can get in sticky situations. I can't leave without Devon anyway because Sage is still here. He has business at In the Mix to tend to, but he refuses to leave the house until Devon arrives. I need Devon to be on time because I have a strict appointment with a lady at the hotel where I want to have my wedding reception. I really love that hotel and want to secure the space as soon as possible.

It is only by fortuitous happenings that I have the possibility of securing the venue. They had a cancellation for the day I need to reserve it for, so I may be able to slide in. My window of opportunity for reserving it is slim, so being late is not an option. Sage may just have to go with me if need be.

"It's almost time for me to leave. I hope your boy isn't gonna be late because I'm not waiting for him. I hope you know. You know I have to have this space reserved today if we're gonna get it," I say to Sage as he walks into the room.

Sage replies, "I know you have to have it and I also know that you aren't going over there without Monster being here. You can say what you want to say, but no more of you just roaming around town by yourself is gonna happen."

I roll my eyes and pop back, "I don't take orders from any man. My father doesn't even dictate what I do, so stop with all of that."

"Listen, I'm not gonna argue with you. You govern yourself. Always have and seemingly always will, but let me put you on to something that's bigger than you. There are two boys named Devin and Deric who need you to humble yourself while we get this situation under control. I'll just leave that right there," Sage voices solemnly and exits the room.

I know my boys need me and that's the only reason why I'm not already out of the door. I'll sit tight and wait for Devon to come this time. Why does Sage always have to throw my boys in my face to get his point across? He knows that he's playing dirty and uses my boys as leverage to make his points transparent. Moments later, the doorbell rings and it's Devon. He's on time as he said he would be. Thank goodness for that. I'm glad Devon is here on time because I hate waiting on people when there's nothing really pressing and when there's something pressing, I despise being delayed exponentially. I grab the boys, our belongings, and head for the door.

We jump in my car and head for the hotel. We pull up to the hotel and Devon helps me get the boys out of the car. I appreciate the fact that he's willing to help me even though I didn't ask him to. I guess he's not going to get paid for just sitting and standing around. We load the boys into their stroller and I push them into the hotel. Surprisingly, Devon grabs their diaper bag and throws it over his shoulder like it's nothing. I know plenty of guys who have children who won't even carry their own children's diaper bag let alone a diaper bag that belongs to someone else. We make it inside the building and I approach the attendant standing at the counter.

"Hello, how can I help you?" the attendant asks pleasantly.

I respond, "Hi, I'm here for an appointment with Mrs. Garcia."

"Thanks, I'll page her for you. You can have a seat over there if you'd like," she speaks.

The attendant pages Mrs. Garcia and Mrs. Garcia promptly comes to where we are seated. We exchange greetings and she tells us to follow her. Mrs. Garcia takes us on a tour of the facility and I have to admit that I'm beyond pleased with what I've seen so far. Now, if the ballroom is as elegant and adequately sized as the pictures online make it seem, it's only a matter of paying for it. Lastly, we end up in the grand ballroom and it's exactly that. It is grand to say the least. I love everything about the space from the tiles on the floor, the crystal chandeliers, and the open concept of the space itself.

I'm in love with the space already and I'm envisioning where I'll be when I have my first dance with Sage as Mrs. Sheena McMillan. I'm more excited than I've ever been about getting married because I'm able to visualize the details now. How lucky am I to be getting married to my best friend? Ooh, I even see a great place for

Sage and me to place the table that we'll light our unity candle on! Yesss, the photographer will be able to focus the camera on us in that quaint space without getting other people in the shot.

Mrs. Garcia finishes telling me about the space and other things that they offer with renting out the space. I listen patiently even though I'm already sold on what I'm going to do. I would interrupt her, but I don't want to be rude. Even Devon is very complimentary about the hotel and its ballroom. Finally, Mrs. Garcia finishes her presentation and asks me what I think about the space. I decide not to tell her how much I'm in love with the ballroom. Instead, I tell her that if the price is right, I'd consider it heavily.

"Let's go to my office and talk about the services you want and how much they will cost you. I have an itemized list of everything we offer along with their costs. I'll be able to give you a quote today," Mrs. Garcia informs.

"Okay, I'd like that. My fiancé will definitely want to know how much this will run him," I reply.

"Yes, they always want to know the bottom line," Mrs. Garcia replies.

We make it back to her office and have a seat. She gives us bottled water as we discuss what services I'm looking for and what they'll cost Sage. Devon entertains the boys while Mrs. Garcia and I conduct business. I'm glad he's keeping them occupied because looking at these numbers and controlling them would be aggravating. The prices of the things I want are a tad bit high to me, but I'm not surprised. Prices for anything related to weddings are always more than they should be. It seems that companies know that the bride wants what she wants desperately, so they take advantage of the situation.

We've discussed everything I want and I now have the grand total of the costs. I know Sage told me that I can have whatever I want, but I still feel the need to run the final cost of the venue through him before I secure it. I excuse myself because I want to call Sage and to make him aware of the final number. Also, I need to use the restroom because that water Mrs. Garcia gave me is about to rupture my bladder. I head to the restroom and call Sage on the way.

He answers the phone and asks, "What's up? How are you making out?"

"Hey, Babe. I'm making out great! I love everything about this venue. I mean it really feels like this is where I'm meant to be married. I knew as soon as I saw the ballroom," I explain.

Sage speaks, "Alright, so it sounds like it's a go. I'm glad that you're excited about the place."

"Yes, I love it. I already started plotting out where we'll dance and everything. I think you'll even like the spot too. However, there is one small problem," I report.

"I'm listening," Sage says.

I speak hesitantly, "Well, the spot is beautiful and has everything I want, but it's pretty expensive and I'll understand if you want me to find another location."

"Expensive is relative to who's speaking and who's receiving the information, so let me judge what's high priced and what is not. What's expensive to a guy making ten dollars an hour may not be expensive to another guy making two hundred dollars an hour. Let me know the price please," Sage orates.

"We really get a lot of stuff with the price, so maybe it isn't so high of a price. We get a free night's stay, wedding coordinator, open bar, and the food is included in the price," I verbalize.

"Sheena, come on. I have to get back to what I'm doing here. I just want to know the price. Stop slow rolling. Time is money; you know that," responds Sage.

"It's right at 35,000 dollars. I know that's a lot, so we can either not do it or we can split it down the middle. If you want, I can just pay the difference between what it costs and what you want to pay," I explain. "I really want to be here!"

"No, we aren't splitting it. Thirty-five grand isn't bad. The way you were acting I thought you were gonna say something astronomical. Just use the credit card I added you on and pay the entire bill. Or you can put a down payment on it, so they hold it for you and I'll write them a check for the remaining balance. It doesn't matter to me one way or the other. Text me to let me know," Sage replies.

"K. Thanks Babe. I will," I say.

Sage ends the call and gets back to his business at the lounge. Needless to say, I'm on cloud nine. No, I'm on cloud ninety-nine. That went way better than I thought it would. I don't know why I thought Sage would trip about the cost because he never trips about spending money. I had my head filled up with a bunch of nothing. I know one thing and it's that my bladder is filled up with something for sure that I need to get rid of.

I need the bathroom now, but I don't know where it is. I begin walking around in search of the bathroom sign. I finally see a sign for the restroom and scutter towards it. I will never wait this long again to use the restroom. Hell, this is sheer torture. What seems like an hour later I finally make it to the restroom. The first three stalls are taken, but the handicapped stall is free, so I jump right in. While I'm in the stall, I feel a great sense of relief overtaking my body which is immediately replaced with fear. I'm relieved because I'm finally relieving my bladder, but the fear inundates my body when I overhear an unusual conversation.

I hear the bathroom door open and then I hear a person walking back and forth as if the person is monitoring the stalls. That's nothing to be alarmed about because I did the exact same thing when I was looking for a stall to use. She obviously walked to see if a stall was available and now she's waiting. A second later, the door opens up again and what I hear is startling.

A lady speaks angrily, "Excuse me sir! You can't be in here. This is the ladies' room and you definitely shouldn't be looking under the stalls at peoples' feet."

"I can use whatever bathroom I want. There's no longer any of that gender stuff. I identify with women more than men and feel comfortable right here. Not that I need to explain myself to you, but I only looked under the stalls to see if there was one available. I'm tired of being discriminated against and living in a closet," he explains.

"Well, that's all fine and dandy, but I don't feel comfortable and I'm sure those women in those stalls wouldn't feel safe knowing that you're in here looking under the stalls. In fact, I'm going to get a manager," she says.

An almost paralyzing fear has gripped my body like the Jaws of Life. I'm struck with fear because I know that voice. It's a voice that will forever be engraved in my head. It's a voice that's synonymous with all things sinister, with all things vile, and with all things wrong with mankind. That's the voice of the devil's agent. I'm sure the man's voice I hear is that of the Uber driver who abducted me. Once the lady states that she's going to get a manager, there's no more dialogue.

Unfortunately, the door never opens up and she's unable to leave the restroom because the guy won't let her. The next thing I hear is what sounds like someone being slapped and then I hear a body splatting on the floor. The ladies in the other stalls also recognize what I do because they let out screams from the sound of the impact. I know he hit her to keep her from exiting the bathroom and telling on him. I immediately pull out my phone in an attempt to call Devon. He's the closest person to this bathroom that I can think of who can help now. I dial his number, but the call won't engage. Damn, why is my phone failing me now? I call him right back and my phone stalls again.

I decide to call 911 even though I know they won't be able to get someone here in time to help me, but I have to inform them of what's going on. He tried to abduct me last time and maybe he'll try again. At least if I call the authorities now, they may be able to get someone here to intercept his plan like Sage did before. How in the hell does he know where I'm going to be and when? To my horror, the 911 call isn't going through either and I don't know why.

The Uber driver screams out, "Ladies in the stalls, I'm not in here to bother all of you. You just happen to be in here at the wrong time. Even though I'm not here to bother all of you, I am here for one of you and she knows who she is. Sheena, come out of the stall and spare these ladies any more fear."

I hate that these ladies are in here with me and are being antagonized because of my conflict, but I'm not coming out of this stall. If I do, I'm a goner and I'm not willing to be gone yet. It's all about self-preservation at this point. I try to call Devon again, but it's to no avail. At this point, my phone is just a projectile that I can use as a weapon if need be. I know I'm scared, but doing nothing isn't going to help me in this situation and isn't an option.

Fortunately, the other women don't come out of their stalls either. I don't know if it's because they don't believe that he won't hurt them or if they're paralyzed with fear and can't move. No matter what their reason is for not moving, I'm just glad they haven't because then he'd know exactly which stall I'm in.

He speaks again, "Ladies, I don't want to kick the stall doors in to see who's in the stall, but I will. If I have to, I'll even shoot into the stall and then you'll surely die, so it's in your best interest to just come out of the stall. I'll count to ten and if you're not out of the stall by then, I'll just do what I have to do."

The women in the stalls are all crying loudly at this point. I should be the one crying because I know that he's here for me, but I'm not crying. I have to strategize my escape out of this perplexing situation. I'm trying to figure out ways to counter whatever moves he may be planning. If he shoots into the stall, what can I do? If he kicks the stall door open and rushes in what can I do? There are too many scenarios to consider. I guess my best option is for him to rush in the stall at me. I stand a better chance of getting away if we have to scuffle than if he shoots me.

My poor body surely can't take getting shot again. My chances of survival would be extremely low. He begins to count down from ten and my mind starts to process what other options I may have. Have I thought of everything? His count is at eight when I hear a lock to a stall unlatch. He stops his count and starts speaking.

"Good for you for unlocking your stall. You're smart for that. Before you come out, I want you to turn around and come out backwards with your eyes closed. It's for your own protection, not mine. If you don't see my face, then I won't have to hurt you. Let's be for real ladies, if I wanted to kill you, I would have killed this lady right here instead of knocking her out. Use your common sense," he states.

It's the lady in the stall beside me who unlatched her stall door. After he gives his instructions on how to exit the stall, the woman exits her stall to his specifications. The guy instructs her verbally to walk over to the corner of the bathroom and put her nose on the wall. She walks with trepidation to the wall, but he doesn't harm her one bit.

He voices, "As you can hear, I didn't harm her because she did what I requested. I'm only here for one person. Sheena, let's end this game. Don't hold these women hostage any longer."

I still don't answer because he'll be alerted to my location once I open my mouth. The guy resumes his count from where he ended previously. I can't stand the sound of his voice and how he seems to be enjoying every second of this. He counts down to six and as he wants it, another stall door becomes unlocked. The girl in the first stall comes from inside and eventually ends up against the wall. I know the other lady is going to exit next, so it's time for me to plan my move.

As I suspected, the next stall door latch is unfastened. I immediately flush the toilet of the stall that I'm in. The lady in the stall walks out backwards just as the other ladies before her did. As she's walking to go take her place on the wall, she begins coughing and sneezing. Seconds later, the other ladies up against the wall and the man holding us hostage begin coughing and sneezing too. The man runs to my stall and gives me a directive to come out, but again I don't respond. He finishes the initial count that he started before and when he's fires several shots into the ceiling.

"Come on out of the stall bitch! Don't make me come in there to get you. Listen, I don't want you dead just yet, but I'll shoot you if I have to.

Don't force my hand," he says angrily.

He's like a man possessed with something I've never seen before. The good thing is that he's still coughing, sneezing, and his eyes are watering profusely. Hell, even my eyes are beginning to bother me. The other women in the bathroom scream at the top of their lungs when they hear the unexpected gun fire. Now is my opportunity to make a run for it. I may not get another chance to make my escape. I hope with the way my eyes are watering, I can get away without bumping into something.

When I flushed the toilet moments ago, I sprayed my pepper spray that I carry in my purse for protection. I needed to mask the sound of me spraying the can, so he wouldn't know what was going on. Before I flushed the toilet, I removed my shirt and dipped it into the toilet to get it wet and then I covered my face with it to keep me from breathing in the pepper spray directly. Doing that mitigated the impact of the spray and gave me the necessary tolerance to make a move. I know that was drastic, but the thought of perishing in a bathroom seemed far worse.

I slid under the bottom of the stall into the empty one beside me when the guy started sneezing and coughing. I knew he'd be disoriented from the pepper spray and wouldn't detect me sneaking into the next stall over. All of those shots he fired were for nothing because they didn't scare me. Next, he kicks in the door of the stall that I was formerly in, expecting to see me cowering in fear. When he inspects the stall and doesn't see my body, his eyes grow huge like the eyes of an owl from astonishment and befuddlement.

He immediately exits the stall and attempts to point his gun in the direction of the other stalls. I know if he starts shooting at the stalls I'm dead, so I exit the stall and rush at him. While running in his direction, I manage to spray him directly in his eyes. Next, I bump him with enough force to knock the gun loose from his hands and the gun falls to the floor. We begin to tussle as we both continue to sneeze and cough. I'm glad I'm in better shape from the effects of the spray than he is because the scuffle would be totally one sided and in his favor. I jump on his back and before I know it, the other ladies in the bathroom help me fight him.

We're too much for him to beat all of us and I think he knows it. Also, I'm sure he's afraid that someone heard the gunshots and is on the way to investigate. He eventually throws me off his back and knocks one girl to the floor and makes his way to the bathroom door and exits. The girls help me up and we also exit the bathroom to get help and hopefully track down the assailant. As we exit the bathroom, Devon comes running up.

"What the hell is going on? Were those gunshots I heard?" Devon asks frantically.

"Yes, those were gunshots. The man who's trying to kill me ended up in the bathroom. We have to call the cops," I respond.

"Damn, I thought those were gunshots. I left the boys in the office with the lady and came looking for you because it seemed to be taking you a long time. Then when I got in the hallway, I heard the shots and I saw a dude running for the staircase," Devon reports.

"That was probably him. Give me your phone. I need to call the cops. I tried calling you when he first trapped us in the bathroom, but it wouldn't dial out. My phone picked the wrong time to act up," I say.

Devon makes his way to the stairwell to see if he can catch up to the guy. I attempt to call the cops again from Devon's phone, but his won't dial out either. Some of the other ladies try to dial from their phones and theirs aren't working either. I zoom to Mrs. Garcia's office to check on my boys and to use her office phone to call the authorities. When I get to her office, she informs me that she heard the ruckus and has already called the police.

We walk back to the bathroom to wait for the cops. The hotel is on lockdown and they're not allowing anyone in or out. About five minutes later, Officer Mosely arrives with other officers and they begin their investigation. The cops examine some items found in the bathroom and one item they retrieve is a cell phone signal blocker. That explains why we were unable to call out from our phones. Additionally, they recover the assailant's gun in the bathroom.

"Ms. Mills, I must say that I'm tired of seeing you in this fashion, but I'm glad to keep seeing you because it means that you're still alive. You're one tough cookie. Hard to kill for sure," states Officer Mosely.

"Yes, I know. Trust that I'm tired of this too. There have been too many life and death situations for me to last a lifetime. I need tranquility in my life," I voice. "I'm blessed to keep coming out of these situations alive. I'm not complaining one bit about that."

Sage has gotten word about what happened and is calling my phone. I talk to him to bring him up to speed on what happened today. He's sorry that it happened, but is thankful that me nor the boys were injured. Unfortunately, since the hotel is on lockdown Sage won't be able to come upstairs when he arrives and I can't leave. He's livid because he'll be stuck standing outside the hotel with all the other spectators. Devon makes it back upstairs a few minutes later. He reports that he was unable to find out where the guy who attacked me and the other women disappeared to.

The guy most likely exited the hotel and made a clean getaway. Unluckily, the guy seems to be a master of escaping sticky situations. The police are very thorough because they still search every floor of the hotel just to ensure that the guy really isn't still in the hotel. After an hour of securing the hotel, the lockdown is lifted and we are able to leave the hotel. I take the boys downstairs to Sage, Ilesha, and Rachel who have been patiently waiting for us.

Sage hugs me and the boys. I'm happy that I'm able to see him again. It really wasn't looking good for me escaping the bathroom, but I did. Rachel and Ilesha are glad to see us too. We enjoy another sisterly embrace as we've done so many times before. My nerves are shot, so I ride home with Sage and Devon drives my car back to the house. Sage and I converse while we drive home.

"I won't sleep well until I get ahead of this. I mean this guy knows where you're going to be seemingly all the time. He has to be following you. That's the only way he can keep ending up where you are," Sage utters. "I was hoping that following up on the Uber records would lead us to the guy, but it didn't. That guy was smart enough to pay someone cash to order the Uber for him, so getting his information that way was a dead end. The guy who actually got paid to order the Uber had never met the guy before."

"I agree with you about being followed, but I can't say that I've noticed anyone following me," I say. "Damn, that sucks about the Uber lead. I thought we would have had him for sure."

Sage words, "You wouldn't know if you were being followed anyway. You don't pay attention to stuff like that. You know you get in your car and don't pay attention to anything other than the speedometer. Either way, I'll get him."

"Well, you know how I do," I reply. "Honey, I know you will. I'm not worried about that."

"Thanks! I wonder if the guy is staking out the house or something. I'll check my surveillance cameras when we get home to see if I see anything that doesn't belong," Sage mentions.

I don't refute what he says because he's right. I normally just get in my car and go. Hell, I have too many other things on my mind to be worrying about what's going on with traffic. I know Sage is really bothered by not being able to catch the person who's harassing my life. He knows that it only takes one time for guy trying to harm me to be successful. We all arrive at the house at virtually the same time and everyone walks inside. Ilesha heads straight for the kitchen and starts fixing alcoholic beverages and Rachel and I take the boys to put them down for a nap. I need something a lot stronger than my normal amaretto sour to sip on after the afternoon I had. Rachel and I discuss the possibilities of how this guy is able to know where I'm going to be and what his motives could be.

CHAPTER 11
Sage's Perspective

As soon as I enter the house, I head straight to my office to check the security cameras that surveillance outside. The only way that guy knows where Sheena will be is if he's following her. If he really is following Sheena, he has to be following her from the house. Every time something happens to Sheena, it's after she leaves the house, so it just makes sense that the person is following her from here. I only have two cameras that have views of street activity and those views are limited because before this I only wanted to record activity that was directed toward my home. Now, I wish I would have thought to put cameras in place to catch more street activity, but I didn't so I'll have to work with what I have.

I rewind my security tape footage to a couple of hours before Sheena left to go to the hotel.

There's a lot of vehicle and pedestrian activity that the cameras catch, but nothing that stands out as being unusual or amiss. I see my neighbors' cars going past, plenty of cars that are just normal traffic, several people walking their dogs, and even people jogging by. Unfortunately, nothing stands out as being ominous and that's a bit frustrating because I'm sure the answer is here, but I just don't know what to look for. Any one of those cars could have been driven by the perpetrator and I wouldn't know. I wish I could see further down the street to see what's going on. I have to adjust the cameras outside to give me more footage.

I head outside to adjust the cameras to provide a broader view of the street activity. It doesn't take long to complete the task. I head inside the house and go back to my office to check the new camera angles. To my delight, I'm able to see much more of the block from the new positioning of the cameras. Hopefully, if that guy is staking out my house, I'll be able to see him and make my move. I have to get him before he gets Sheena. He's already had more chances at taking Sheena's life than I'm comfortable with. Once again, I can't wait for the police to handle this. I have to rectify this situation myself and I will.

There must be something on these recordings. Maybe I need to go back a little further to catch somebody slipping. The person would have no way of knowing he was being videotaped, so he may have been sloppy. I go back to yesterday's footage to see if I see something that doesn't belong. Here we go again! It's the same nothingness as earlier today. There goes the neighbor's car, people jogging, and people walking their dogs. Oh well, I guess I have to rely on the camera changes I've made to find out something further.

Wait! Who the hell is this guy who seems to be staring at the house? Why did he slow down and take so much interest in my house. I know he has no business peering at my house like that. I zoom in to see if I can get a better picture of his face. Oh yeah, that's a perfect shot! I got his ass now! I don't recognize him, but maybe Sheena will. He doesn't fit the description of the guy Sheena described as her attacker, but he could surely be working with him. Two people working together would really be able to throw the police off the trail.

"Sheena, come here!" I call out.

Unfortunately, she doesn't respond, so I call out for her once more. I guess she's too busy being loud and having drinks with her girls to hear me calling her. I leave my office to go get her, so she can inspect the tape. When I walk into the living room, Sheena is just ending a phone call. Sheena has calmed down from the incident and is excited about something. How she changes so quickly from one emotion to the next is beyond me. Maybe the drinks have loosened her up. She knows she puts them down when she gets with her girls. I decide to investigate why there's such a drastic change in Sheena's demeanor.

"What has you so happy now? Was that the cops saying they caught the guy or something?" I inquire.

"No, that was Mrs. Garcia from the hotel that we're getting married at. She called to apologize about what happened to me down there. Apparently, she felt so badly about it that she decided to cut the cost of ballroom in half," Sheena reports happily.

Rachel inserts, "That was very nice of her. She really didn't have to do that. Now, that's great customer service."

Ilesha chimes in, "Girl, please. Hell no it ain't! I'm sure her superiors at the hotel heard about the incident and figured that this is the best way to keep from getting their asses sued. Don't fall for that nice and caring routine."

"Hell, I don't care if she's genuinely sorry or if her superiors told her to discount the venue. Now what I do care about is the bottom line and the bottom line is that I'm being discounted fifty percent of the total cost," Sheena vocalizes with a hint of arrogance.

"That's good, but don't forget that you actually aren't paying for anything. I'm fitting the bill on this one and I'll take fifty percent off any day," I comment.

"I know, but you know what I'm saying. You know I love a discount. It's always good to feel like you're getting something for free," Sheena remarks.

"I know that's right. I can't pass up a sale on some new shoes. It's like you just can't leave them in the store when it's such a good deal," Rachel voices.

"Enough about these shoes. You almost made me forget what I came out here for. I have the surveillance video of outside the house pulled up and there's a strange dude on the footage who's paying an awful lot of attention to the house. I don't recognize the guy at all, so I want you to take a look at him to see if you know him," I explain.

"Show me. Come on y'all. I want you two to look at him too. If I don't recognize him, maybe one or both of you will," Sheena utters.

We all head to my office to look at the footage. I let the camera roll until the guy walks into the frame and then I freeze it. They all agree that it's strange the way he peers at the house as if he's looking for something. None of them can tell who he is at first, but they can clearly see that the guy isn't the Uber driver who kidnapped Sheena. Next, I zoom in on the guy's face and Sheena immediately is moved by the still shot of him.

"I know that fucker! That's Eric's cousin

Dion. I first met him at Eric's birthday party. Those two were like brothers, but he's definitely not the guy who was driving the Uber car or who was in the bathroom," Sheena informs.

"I agree he's not the Uber driver for sure. It's possible that he's working with someone though. You never know. People are crazy out here these days," Rachel mentions.

"I know that's right. These men have been tripping over me for putting this good-good on them for years. Girl, when I would take it away they would damn near starve themselves to death from being so miserable. Men are crazy as hell! You have to watch them," Ilesha chimes in.

"What's his last name?" I ask angrily.

"I don't know for sure, but I can find out," Sheena answers.

Sheena swiftly runs out of the office and returns with her iPad and accesses a file on it. Apparently, she has the names of all of the people who attended Eric's party in the file. She has Dion's full name in the matter of seconds.

"Burns is his last name. Dion Burns is his full name. I thought that was his last name, but I wanted to be sure," I report.

I take Sheena's iPad to see exactly how his name is spelled and punch it into Facebook. Regrettably, there are dozens of Dion Burns out here. I don't want to have to look through all of these names to find him, but I will if I have to. After thumbing through about fifty Dion Burns who aren't the one I'm looking for, I decide to try another route.

"Sheena, do you know if Eric's Facebook page is still up and running?" I inquire.

"I don't know because I blocked him on all social media because he was tripping with the messages, but I doubt it's shut down because people normally leave them up. Just type his name in and see what pops up," Sheena answers.

I type in Eric's name and luckily his page on Facebook is still active. I look through his friend list and find Dion's name in seconds. This is definitely the same person. I'm going to get to the bottom of why he's outside of my damn house.

"We need to call the cops and let them know that Dion has been outside your house. I'm sure they'll be plenty interested in knowing why he's on your block. He can't just stalk Sheena and have no consequence," Rachel words.

"We can call the cops and tell them that Dion is on my block. That's not a crime because this is a public street and he can walk wherever he wants. It's a free country for the most part," I vocalize.

"His ass will fuck around and be cut up if I'm around while he's out here lurking," Ilesha assures.

"I know you will slice him the first chance you get. I wonder what the hell he's out here for. This is crazy, I mean like really crazy," Sheena states. "Sage is right though. Walking down a street looking at houses is no crime."

Devon speaks while pounding his fist into his other hand, "Listen, I know one thing and that's if I see him by this house, I'm snatching him up. No questions asked."

I say, "The way it looks is that Dion and the Uber driver are working together. Dion is probably upset about the way things went with Eric and now wants you dead. He scopes out the house and then relays when you leave to the other guy. We just have to figure out who the other guy is. Once we do that, we'll be able to end it just like we did with Eric and Kevin. We have the upper hand because they don't know that we know Dion is involved."

"Sage, are you going to set them up like you did Eric and Kevin?" Rachel asks.

"I'll do whatever I have to do to protect my family, but my plan is just to find the other guy and have him arrested. There's been too much violence and bloodshed for a lifetime lately," I explain.

"Okay, because I don't want to be involved with another murderous scheme. Sending them to jail is an adequate punishment for what they are doing," Rachel voices.

I reply, "I understand. Nah, no murder plots this time. We'll keep the police abreast of what's going on when we need to and let them handle their business."

"Whatever works Babe. If it keeps us safe, I'm all for it. I just want to be able to enjoy life without the threat of harm to me and my loved ones," Sheena asserts.

"I'm so glad you feel that way because I think we need to postpone the wedding until this entire fiasco is settled. A wedding takes a lot of planning and will require you to be out a lot, so it's best we wait on the wedding. You become vulnerable when you're out and about," I suggest.

Sheena screams, "You must be out of your damn mind! Ain't no way in hell that I'm postponing, cancelling, changing the time or altering any one detail about my wedding! This is my day and I'm not letting anyone mess it up. The way I see it is that you better do your job as the man and protect your family from harm. I can't believe you said that to me just now."

I don't know what I was thinking by suggesting that to Sheena. She's already sent out the save the dates to all of her friends and family and would be terribly embarrassed if she recanted now. I guess the earful she just gave me is warranted. I should have thought better of my words before I shared them. She's right; it is her day. Furthermore, it's my job to guard my family and I'll do just that.

I decide that I need to get away from Sheena for a minute to let her calm down. I need to go to the hotel to pay for the venue anyway, so there's no better time than now. I let them know that I'm stepping out to handle some business. I decide not to tell Sheena what I'm doing because I want to surprise her. I need something to help calm her down. Looks like I'll be going to the store to pick up some fresh flowers for her.

CHAPTER 12
Sheena's Perspective

I need to talk to my girls in private, so I have them come to my bedroom. I don't want Devon to overhear what we talk about. Not that it's anything bad, but I like to talk freely without outside people hearing what I'm saying. We make it to my room and I close the door behind us.

"Girl, that shit about postponing the wedding lit a fire under me. I almost became someone else. Sage had me hot. It took the strength of the world to keep me from slapping him," I say.

"I was hoping you slapped him. I told myself once you started yelling at him that if you swung I was too. Talking about being vulnerable. Don't nobody got time for that," Ilesha states.

Rachel remarks, "I'm so glad you didn't hit him because we already have drama in the streets and the last thing we need is drama in the house. I do think he was severely out of line by suggesting that you postpone the wedding. That was poor taste on his part. I would have thought that he'd know better than that by now. Well, he is a man and I don't think most men really understand how important marriage is to us."

"Yes, we don't need any more drama and that's why I didn't go over the top on him. I just let him know sternly that I wasn't having any delays on my wedding. I got my point across and didn't need to put hands on him, but thanks for having my back," I speak.

"You definitely did that. You know you are my 'she-ro' and always have been," replies Ilesha.

Rachel and Ilesha decide it's time for them to leave. They've been out longer than they anticipated and want to get to their respective homes. As always, I'm glad that my girls came to check on me after the hotel incident. I'm forever grateful for them. I'm blessed with two perfect boys, an ambitious fiancé, and two excellent best friends. Rachel is off from work tomorrow and is begging me to let her keep the boys for a sleep over. I jump all over the opportunity and expeditiously get the boys ready to go. After the day I've had, I really need the night to kick back and not worry about being a mom.

We all say our goodbyes and they pull off. It's even better that Rachel took the boys with her because now I can run out in the morning. I wasn't going to leave the house tomorrow because I didn't want to lug the boys around, but that's no longer the case. I'll be able to move easier without the boys. I tell Devon that I'm in for the night, so he can leave. He informs me that Sage asked him not to leave until he returns and that he'll just chill in the living room until Sage gets back. I don't have a problem with that, but I'm not keeping him company. I go upstairs and chill while I'm entertained by social media. An hour later, Sage returns home and Devon is about to leave. I'm glad I came downstairs because I need Devon to be back here at ten in the morning, so I can run some errands without the boys. Devon agrees to be here at ten and then departs for the night.

Sage has flowers for me. They smell great and are beautiful. I act like they don't really mean that much to me. I can't just let him walk in here and win me over just like that. I have to play hard to get for a little while. He has to know that he was out of line with his suggestion of postponing the wedding. I don't even engage the flowers and instead I have him put the flowers in water himself. I walk upstairs to the bedroom and sit on the ottoman. A few minutes later, Sage comes upstairs and enters the room.

"So, what are you supposed to be mad or something?" Sage asks.

"No, I'm not mad, so I don't know where you're getting that notion from. You must know you said some bullshit earlier and think that I should be mad," I respond.

"Yeah, I was a little off base with the wedding postponement, but it was only suggested to keep you safe. It wasn't meant to slight you in any way, shape, or form. I hope you don't think I said to postpone it to escape marrying you. Baby, I want to marry you and that'll never change. It's always been you and only you," Sage narrates.

"Is that a fact?" I ask.

"Yes, it's incontrovertible. You can look it up online if you want to," Sage says.

"I don't believe everything that's on the internet, so you have to do better than that. You have to come harder than that. I know you can do better," I urge.

"I can definitely 'cum' harder than that and you're gonna find out tonight," Sage replies in a mannish fashion.

Sage goes into the bathroom and starts running the Jacuzzi. After he runs the Jacuzzi water, he goes downstairs and grabs some wine. He knows I've already been drinking today and knows that my horniness will be very high with anymore alcohol. For some reason, I think that's his plan. He wants me tipsy, so he can take advantage of me sexually. I have no problem with that. Sage makes it back with the wine and some glasses. He goes straight for the music when he returns.

We sip the wine while the Jacuzzi fills up.

Sage strips me down slowly and seductively as the soft music plays in the backdrop. I feel myself becoming hot and bothered from the wine and the way Sage touches me as he undresses me. I gently twirl my body to the music as I become more intoxicated. I'm quickly stark naked in the bedroom and Sage carries me to the Jacuzzi while he kisses me. He leans over and places me into the bubbling Jacuzzi water. Sage's brown barrel-chested body is fully exposed in front of me. He glides into the Jacuzzi and sits in front of me. My supple breasts are pressed up against his back while my arms are wrapped around his waist.

I lick his neck and smoothly move my tongue across the back of his neck to his ear and nibble on it. I reach down and rub my fingers through his pubic hair. Then I begin to stroke Sage's dick as I sit behind him until it's fully hard. He turns his head and looks over his shoulder at me and protrudes his lips for me to kiss and I do just that. I peck Sage's lips and then I peck them again. When I go to peck his plump lips again he pulls back. I love being teased and Sage knows that for sure. I lean forward again to get my kiss and Sage meets me. Our lips meet for a passionate kiss. Our kiss is a mixture of tongues swirling and bottom lip sucking. I stand up over Sage because I want to sit on his lap while we embrace and kiss, but I'm stopped as I step over him.

Sage grabs me as I spread my legs to step over

him and rubs my clit. I stand tranquil with my legs wide open while he massages my coochie. He grabs my ass cheek with one hand and with the other continues stimulating my pussy. The feeling is starting to get overwhelming and I whirl my body to the motion of his touch.

"Yes, Baby," I moan. "Just like that."

I run my hands through my hair and pinch my erect nipples. Sage motions me to sit down, so I sit on the edge of the Jacuzzi and spread my legs almost to the point of a full split. Sage grabs my foot and rests it on his chest. He massages my ankle and foot and then begins sucking my toes. Sage then smooches and licks my leg and inner thigh until he reaches my treasure chest. He enters my pussy with his tongue and navigates my insides like a captain navigating the sea.

I raise my hands above my head and brace myself on the wall. I push my body forward to Sage's face while he eats me out. Oh, his tongue is amazing and masterful! It almost feels like he has two tongues working on me. Sage knows how to make my body cream. I twirl on Sage's face like a belly dancer. I wrap my legs around his head and he continues to slurp on my sweet spot. Sage goes from eating my pussy in a kneeling position to grabbing both my ass cheeks and lifting me up in the air while he tastes my punani. I gyrate on his face and my body gets extremely hot and tingly. I release what feels like a small explosion in his mouth. The orgasm is so intense that I'm lightheaded. Sage has taken me to a sexual place I've never been before. I'm amazed that Sage continues to have so many tricks in his repertoire.

Sage sits me back on the edge of the Jacuzzi and takes my silk head scarf off of my head. He ties my hands together and goes back to eating me out. The feeling is almost too good to the point where I want to push him away, but I can't because my hands are tied. All I can do is squirm and moan as he licks all over me. He stops eating me out and looks up at me with my pussy juice all over him. Fuck, I'm turned on by how freaky he is. Sage grabs one of my breasts with both hands and sucks my titty and swirls his tongue around my areola. He kisses me romantically while caressing my body.

He picks me up and places me back into the Jacuzzi. Sage rests his dick on my breasts and then places his dick between both of them. My man gently squeezes my boobs together around his dick and titty fucks me. His dick is so long that it's protruding into my face, so I stick my tongue out in an effort to lick it.

"Oh, you want to taste him?" Sage asks.

I nod my head to certify that I want to suck his dick. Sage stops titty fucking me and tells me to stick my tongue out. I extend my tongue out of my mouth and he seductively plops his dick on it. As I lick the head of his dick, he steps forward so his balls are almost touching my lips. I open my mouth wide and Sage slowly inserts his cock into my mouth and then pulls it out. He erotically rubs his dick on my face and then sticks it back in my mouth slowly. I close my eyes and wrap my warm mouth around his dick and begin sucking it. He grips my shoulders as he pumps my face. His dick penetrates my throat so deeply that I gag on it. His rod is banging my tonsils like a boxer punching a punching bag. Sage is in complete control because my hands are still bound and I love it.

His pumps get faster and faster and water begins to splash in my face, but I don't flinch. I continue slobbering over his dick just as he likes. I'm filled with desire and lust. Sage pops his dick out of my mouth and directs me to lie back on the top surface of the Jacuzzi. Right now, I'm his sex slave, so I do as I'm told. I lean back and Sage takes is thick brown dick and rubs it in circles on my clit. He's teasing me, but this time I want him to stop. I want him to penetrate my walls right now and give me the hard fucking I want. If my hands weren't tied, I'd reach down and stuff his cock into my pussy myself.

He stops rubbing his dick on my clit and puts it inside of me. He fills my walls with his elongated dick and slowly gives me the business. I moan and angle my body to receive as much of his dick as I can. I love the way he surfs my insides. Sage runs his finger along the crack of my ass and fondles my asshole. The new sensation adds more delight and sends tingles from the top of my head to the bottom of my feet.

"Yasss, I like that. Don't stop," I utter.

In, out, round and round his dick goes. He's banging my walls, seemingly penetrating my stomach, and tickling my asshole. This dick is so good that I want to bottle it up and make sure it never gets away. I'm moaning, biting my lips, my eyes are rolling, and I'm cumming all over his dick. My body tremors violently like I'm having a seizure. Sage holds me tenderly and allows me to take in every moment of pleasure.

"Put it in my ass," I order.

Sage stops rubbing my asshole with his thumb and puts his thumb in my ass. The feeling is lovely and I want more. Sage reads my mind and switches fingers and stuffs his middle finger in me. His finger reaches farther than his thumb and provides more euphoria. I pump his finger harder than I did his thumb. I'm sexually stimulated more and more with each stroke of his finger. Why haven't I tried anal sex in the past? This shit is the bomb dot com!

"Baby, I want to ride him now," I say in a low seductive voice.

Sage removes his finger from my ass and slides down into the Jacuzzi almost fully submerged. I sliver down into the water after him. Sage unties my hands and I reach into the water to stroke his rod. Now, it's time for me to serve my king. His dick is bulging hard and it's my job to get it limp like a cooked spaghetti noodle. Sage is sitting with his back against the Jacuzzi with his arms outstretched like Al Pacino in "Scarface". It's like he's saying that I'm his for the taking.

I'm going to do just that! I ease to my man and rub his muscle-bound chest. I climb on top of him and we kiss like only lovers do. I reach down into the water and get a firm grip on his dick and lift myself up to insert it inside me. I ease myself down on as much of his dick as I can handle and begin to work my pussy up and down on his cane. He has a tight grip on my waist and licks my tits as we make passionate love.

"I want you to fuck me in my ass. Will you do that for me, Baby?" I ask.

Sage doesn't answer and nods his head to indicate yes. I continue to wind and grind on him. He pulls me in close to him like he's bear hugging me. Even though I'm on top, he takes control of me. Instead of me surfing his dick, he holds me still in a tight snuggle and drops his body down lower in the water. He takes his dick out of my pussy and puts the head of his dick in my ass. It seems like his dick is too wide to fit inside of me, so I take a deep breath and begin to push out since my asshole is so tight. He slowly inches his dick into my ass as I continue to push to help the process. I don't move any other part of my body and actually tense up because it's such a tight squeeze. Just having the tip of his dick in my ass is jubilation. I carefully and slowly ease more of his dick inside of my ass until I can't bear anymore. Sage begins to deliver short jabs to my ass and I love it. More and more of his dick is in my ass after each stroke.

I bounce my ass back on his dick. Now, I'm riding his dick like he's in my pussy. We are creating more motion in the water than the jets in the tub. I'm screaming, Sage is grunting, and my asshole is stretched wider than I ever thought it could be. Sage's jabs are now long hard strokes into my ass. I'm crying because it feels so good. I feel Sage's dick get bigger in my ass. He's almost there and grabs me tighter than he already is and rough housing me. He lets out the roar of a lion as he releases his load in my ass. I'm breathing heavily and crying from the fucking I've received.

Sage loses all aggression and tenacity that he once possessed. His arms that were once gripping me have lost all of their might and are now lifeless in the Jacuzzi tub. Sage and I cuddle as I think about how amazing that was. I'm tickled to think how he's all mine. We get out of the tub after a half hour of cuddling and take a couple's shower. After the shower, we get in bed and fall asleep.

It's morning and Sage is already up and about. He desires to have the lounge open soon, so he has to get there to ensure plans are on schedule. I'm still in the bed even though I need to get up.

I have to make a few calls to some clients, handle a few errands related to the wedding, and stop by my office. Why can I still feel Sage's dick in my ass? I feel like I'm still open. I hope my asshole closes back up soon. This is crazy! I'm still leaking his cum out of my ass. I didn't sign up for all of this, but I am hoping to do it again.

Sage brings me breakfast in bed, gives me a kiss goodbye, and heads for the door. How sweet of him to make sure I'm straight before he leaves for the day? I think I turned him out last night with my new level of freakiness. He didn't know what hit him. Wait, he's leaving before Devon gets here? I must have really put it on him because he's not thinking straight.

"Honey, I'll text you later. Hit me up if you need anything," Sage says.

"Thank you for breakfast and I will," I reply.

"For your info, Devon is downstairs in the kitchen eating breakfast and is ready to go whenever you are. I'm outta here," Sage informs.

Well, maybe I didn't put it on him as much as I thought because he's clearly still in his right mind. No, I'm tripping. I gave his ass the business last night. He was sleeping like he was in a coma last night. Alright Sheena, time to get yourself together. I finish my breakfast and drag myself out of bed and shower. Yesss, this shower is life right now! I finish showering, get dressed, and head downstairs.

"Good morning Devon," I say.

"Morning. It's hot as hell outside already," Devon replies while shaking his head in disbelief of the early morning temperature.

I ask, "It's hot like that already?"

"Listen, you're gonna start sweating as soon as the air touches your skin. It's crazy like that already," Devon reports.

"Damn, I feel you. Let's roll then. Ain't no reason to delay," I speak.

We head to the garage and jump in the car. I pop the garage door and back out of the garage. I clear the garage and notice the garbage can is blocking the path of the car. Today isn't garbage day. I mention to Devon that the trash can is in the way and he tells me that he'll move it. I really don't want to get out in the heat that he spoke about. Devon is such a gentleman and I see why Sage hired him. He's always on time and takes his job seriously.

Devon gets out of the car and moves the garbage can. He moves the can and heads back to the passenger's side to get in. He opens the door and as he steps in to sit down, he gets struck in the head with a two by four. I scream in astonishment because the last thing I expected was for this to happen. I guess at this point in my life I should expect the unexpected. Devon is unable to turn around to defend himself and is hit by the two by four one more time and slumps over in the seat. I believe he's unconscious. I want to throw the car in reverse, but if I do, I'll run Devon over for sure. The person responsible for hitting Devon is the Uber driver who abducted me and he's looking me square in my face.

I reach to take my seatbelt off, so I can make a run for it. The Uber driver takes out his stun gun and aims it at me. There is no way that I'll be able to dodge the stun gun prongs and take my seatbelt off at the same time. I have to throw the car in reverse. Hell, it's either Devon getting hurt or I get hurt and I choose Devon. I reach for the gear shift as the man pulls the trigger. Fortunately, at the same time he pulls the trigger, Devon summons some energy and kicks the guy's leg and throws him off balance causing the stun gun prongs to go towards the windshield.

I throw the car in reverse and back out of the driveway. I hoped it wouldn't go this way, but Devon falls out of the car and hits his head. It could have been worse because I didn't run him over which was very likely to happen. I floor it out of the driveway without checking to see if any cars are coming. Sadly, my timing is no good because I hit a car as I back into the street. Obviously, the car stalls for a second. That short pause before I'm able to put the car in drive to pull off gives my attacker enough time to run over to the car. As I'm putting the car in drive to pull off and make my getaway, my attacker opens the passenger's side door and tries to jump in the car.

I look over in surprise and wonder why I didn't lock the door, but that's not going to help me now. I spray my mace just as his butt makes it to the seat of the car. He is discernably impacted by the mace, but so am I. The car is in drive, but the mace has my vision a tad blurred and I can't see as well as I would like. We tussle as I drive and we both try to fight off the impact of the spray. I eventually crash my car into one of the parked cars on the street. In my favor, the car crashes on his side of the car, so he can't open the door. I open my door and try to make a run for the house, but the assailant grabs my blouse and slows me down. I scratch him down his face and he lets out a squeal of pain. I break free from his grasp and make my dash to the house.

My eyes are still a little bothered, but I'm able to make my way towards the house. I look at the car as I'm running past and see the guy try to open the passenger's door to no success. He realizes the door is pinned against the car I hit and begins climbing over to the driver's side of the car to exit. I know I don't have long to get in the house before he's on me, so I have to be swift. I decide not to run in the garage because I don't want to get trapped in there. Instead, I run up the steps to enter the house from the front door.

CHAPTER 13
Sheena's Perspective

Just as I feared, the Uber driver is heading this way. I'm filled with a sense of urgency that I've only felt a few times in my life, but I refuse to panic and drop my keys. I pull on the screen door, but it's locked. Damn! I don't have the time to find the key for the screen door, open it, then unlock and open the wooden door to the house before he makes it over here. My adrenaline is pumping. I yank the screen door handle and it flies open. I have my key ready to open the door to the house, but I only will have time to unlock the door before this man makes it to me. I can't risk opening the door and then getting trapped in the house with him again. Last time, I only lived because Sage made it home just in time to save me.

The guy is coming up the steps, so it's either fight or flight for me. I run down from the top of the stairs toward him. He stops making his way up the stairs seemingly to brace for my charge. He plants his feet and takes a defensive stance, but it's all for nothing. I make it to the landing between the two flights of stairs and jump off the side of the porch. I choose to flee because I know I can't take him in a head to head battle. I have to be realistic about my abilities and chances to succeed in my present predicament.

I jump over the rail like Gale Devers used to jump hurdles and start running even before my feet hit the ground. Where are the neighbors when you need them? The Uber driver has a stunned look on his face when he sees me sailing over the rail. He promptly runs down the few stairs he initially went up and the chase is on. I try to run for the sidewalk, but he's a lot faster than I am and closes off the possibility of me making it to the sidewalk. I hate that I have to run in the backyard because there's less of a chance of me getting away. I need all of that running on the treadmill to help me now.

I run to the backyard and just as expected, he follows behind me. What am I going to do? I don't have anywhere to hide. Hell, I'll just run around the house and come out on the other side. With him behind me, I'll have an unobstructed path to the sidewalk and street and I'll surely be able to get help then. I run as fast and as hard I can to get around the house. To my good fortune and the blessings of God, I make it to the other side of the house without him catching up to me. I'm out of breath, but seeing a clear path to the streets invigorates me to keep pushing forward.

I run full speed ahead toward the street. To my horror, my attacker jumps out in front of me and grabs me. Where in the hell did he come from? Clearly, he turned around and went back the other way to cut me off. He has me right where he wants me. I'm in his grasp and in a secluded area. He grabs me by the neck and lifts me in the air choking me. I kick and flail, but nothing is deterring him from accomplishing his mission. He pins me up against the side of the house while he chokes the life out of my body.

He's shaking and banging me up against the house while he continues to choke me. Out of nowhere, Devon comes to my rescue. Devon swings the same two by four that he was assaulted with at my attacker. Sadly, he sees it coming and drops me before it hits him. He's able to duck out of the way and put up a fight. I take a second to gather myself before I get up and run to get help. Devon takes another swing at the man as I run to the street to. I left my phone in the car, so I'm heading to the car to get it to call the authorities.

Gladly, when I make it to the front of the house, I see a cop tending to the lady who was in the car I crashed into when I backed out of the driveway. I run over to him shouting that the man who attacked me is on the side of the house. Before I'm able to tell the cop all of the details, he draws his gun and moves with a sense of urgency in the direction of the side of the house to capture the criminal. He tells me to stand back while he handles his business. I decide to go to the car to get my phone to call Sage.

As I'm returning from getting my phone, I see the officer coming from the side of the house with a man in handcuffs. Angrily, I see that the cop grabbed the wrong man. The policeman has Devon in restraints instead of my attacker. What went wrong over there? Maybe he has the other guy detained on the side of the house because he was unsure who was who, so he put both of them in restraints until he was able to sort things out. I need to find out what's really going on.

"Wait, wait. Officer, you grabbed the wrong guy!" I state assertively.

The officer replies, "Ma'am, I'm confused. You said the guy on the side of the house was the one who was attacking you, so I went to the side of the house and this man was the only one who was over there."

"I don't know what happened to him. He was there when I left from over there. Devon is my bodyguard and not the attacker. He can fill us in on what happened," I voice.

The cop takes the cuffs off of Devon and Devon begins to tell his story. As he's telling the story, an ambulance pulls up to treat the lady who

I rammed into. Officer Mosely arrives at the same time as the other units do. They approach us to hear what's going on.

Devon explains, "We were on the side of the house when Sheena ran off. I was holding the two by four and he was standing in front of me with his dukes up. I swung the two by four at him and missed. Then, he punched me in the face. Next, I hit him in the stomach with the two by four and he stumbled back. I ran at him, swung, and hit him again on the side of his head. We both heard Sheena call for the officer and that's when he took off in the other direction. He jumped the fence and I went chasing after him, but that's when the officer said freeze and for me to get on the ground. I complied, but was trying to tell him what was going on, but he cuffed me instead. After that, he began escorting me up front and that's when you saw us."

Some of the cops rush the backyard to canvas the area. My attacker has a huge head start on them. He probably will escape again like he always does. I tell the cops the story from start to finish of what happened. They conduct their investigation like always. I'm tired of investigations and I'm ready for results. Officer Mosely tells me that the fingerprints they lifted from the bathroom at the hotel also match the guy's prints from the night I was attacked at my old house and the Uber driver's prints. I could have told him that. I thank the officer and they all leave just as Sage is pulling up. Sage rushes to me, hugs me, and places a firm kiss in the top of my head.

"Okay, this shit is infuriating me! This guy is pretty damn intent on hurting you. Baby, I'm sorry. I just don't know what to say past that. I'm going to handle this. I promise. Fuck! The cops aren't moving fast enough for me. I just have to figure out how to end this," Sage verbalizes.

I tell the entire story to Sage as we sit in the living room. He lets me tell my side of things and then we go to his office to look at the security video. Sage, Devon, and I all watch the entire situation unfold. It's almost like watching a movie. The video shows the guy put the garbage can behind the car. It appears that it was a ruse to get me out of the car. It's a good thing Devon got out instead of me. I would have been finished especially if I was alone. Sage cringes at all of the close calls that took place today.

The video has a clear-cut shot of the guy's face who's after me. Sage saves a picture of the guy to his computer and emails it to Officer Mosely. Next, he calls Officer Mosely to alert him of the photo. Officer Mosely tells him that he'll check the photo when he gets back to the station and that he'll do what needs to be done with it. Sage apologizes to Devon for the injuries he's suffered, but praises him for saving my life. Devon leaves to go get checked out. I'll be forever indebted to

Devon for saving my life. Sage and I look at the tape some more in utter disbelief. Sage gets madder and madder every time he plays it back.

CHAPTER 14
Sage's Perspective

I keep looking back at the security footage to see if I can gleam anything from the tape. We dodged another tragedy today, but I know that we can't rely on getting lucky all the time. Me or the police have to stop this guy before he's successful in his endeavor. I hope now that we've given a picture of the guy to the authorities that they can circulate the picture and get his identification. With all of the social media out here, somebody will recognize him. It's only a matter of time.

I can see when the guy comes walking from down the street and appears in the camera shot. He's clearly staking out the house and is very careful about his movements. I'm glad my boys weren't with Sheena during the altercation. If he hurts a hair on my boys' heads, I'm going to lose my mind and will stop at nothing to find this guy and destroy him. Devon really came through for me today by saving Sheena's life. Hiring him is the best money I've ever spent in my life.

Alright, I've seen enough of the security footage, so I close it down. It's time to strategize all of the things I have going on. Protect Sheena's life, raise my boys, reopen the lounge, and plan a wedding are all things that I have to do, so my focus can't wane for a moment. I am capable of handling all of them successfully. I've been in adverse situations plenty of times and I've always come out on top and I don't expect now to be any different.

I go online to check Dion's Facebook account to see if I can see where he is. I'm hoping he's the type of person who shares his every move with the world. It would be lovely for him to be checked in somewhere. Dion Burns let me know something. Where the hell are you? Damn! His page is only open to his friends, so I can't see any of his activity. I wonder if he has an Instagram account.

I hit the Instagram app in to see if I can catch up to Eric's cousin Dion. I search his name, but nothing comes up. For all I know he is on Instagram, but isn't using his government issued name. I wish Sheena knew more about him. If she knew where he works that would be a great help, but she doesn't. I don't want to mention Dion to the cops because they may tip him off to us being onto him and that may prevent us from ultimately getting to Sheena's attacker.

Wait! Dion is Eric's cousin and they seem to have been pretty close while Eric was alive, so it's likely that Dion was at the celebration Eric had at In the Mix when the boys were born. If so, he has to be following In the Mix on Facebook, Twitter, and Instagram because it was a requirement of anyone in their party. I never missed an opportunity to boost the lounge's exposure. I log into my lounge's account and search for Dion's name. Yes! Just as I suspected, Dion is following the lounge. Now, let me check his wall and see what I see. Where do you work? Where are you going to be?

Okay, so Dion works at an engineering company on the other side of town. This is good information to know. Also, it looks like he's a member at Silver's Gym in DuPont Circle. Now, we are getting somewhere because I can use this information to follow him if need be. Another great thing is that Dion does like many people do and posts his whereabouts often, so I'll be able to keep a tab on him easily. In fact, he's at the gym right now.

Sheena comes over to me to see what I have going on. She hugs me from behind and I show her that I was able to get the information I wanted pertaining to Dion. I see that Dion drives a brand new Impala with all the bells and whistles. He won't be hard to spot with those rims on it. I look back at the security camera from around the time Dion was in front of the house and surely notice the Impala drive past. I have one piece of the puzzle down, but have many more to go.

"You feel like taking a ride?" I ask Sheena.

"Yeah, I'm down, but I do have to pick the boys up from Rachel in a little while. Let me go put my shoes on and I'll be ready in a few minutes," Sheena replies.

"True, I know your few minutes are really like twenty minutes, so I'll be downstairs waiting for you. Just let me know when you're ready," I say comically.

"Whatever," Sheena says as she slaps my arm and goes to get ready.

I grab my gun and go downstairs to wait for Sheena. She comes downstairs twenty minutes later looking like she's about to hit the catwalk. Why am I not surprised? Sheena doesn't leave the house if she's not in tip top form. She's always been like that and it looks like she'll always remain that way. I shake my head and smile as I get up to exit the house.

"What's so funny?" Sheena inquires.

I play dumb and don't offer up a comment as to why I'm smiling. I'd rather her always look her best than to come out the house looking raggedy and disheveled. Sheena is America's next top model. We jump in the car and drive over to the gym where Dion has a membership. We arrive at the gym and drive around the parking lot until we spot the car. I pull into a parking space that gives us a clear view of Dion's car.

We sit in the car for about thirty minutes and finally we see Dion come out of the gym. He gets in his car and drives off. We pull out the space we're in and follow behind him. I do my best to keep a far enough distance from him to keep us from being detected. About fifteen minutes later, Dion pulls into an apartment complex, parks his car, and goes into one of the units. Now, I know where he lives, so I can follow him when I want to. Sheena and I leave the apartment complex. While we're driving back, Sheena calls Rachel to let her know that we're coming to pick the boys up.

"This is crazy! Dion's been outside our house for no justifiable reason, my attacker has been to our house, and Marcus made some ominous statements to me too. This is unreal. I just don't feel safe," Sheena voices.

"Marcus? What are you talking about Marcus? Who is Marcus and what did he say to you?" I ask angrily.

"Marcus is a guy me and my girls met at an all-white party before the boys were born. He tried to holla at me, but it turned out he was married, so we clowned him. He was a little angry, but nothing major. Anyhow, the day I got kidnapped at the mall, Marcus bumped into us and told me that I was gonna get mine and bad karma was coming my way," Sheena reports.

"And you forgot to mention this to me and the cops? How could you forget to mention something so important? Don't you know this information adds a whole new dynamic to the situation?" I ask.

"I'm sorry, but with all that happened that day, Marcus was out of sight and out of mind. It didn't come back to me until just now. I can't imagine that he'd really try to hurt me over me and my girls clowning him one night almost two years ago," Sheena verbalizes.

"Sheena, I know you've been through a lot lately, so it's understandable. Going forward, I need to know any and everything about what happens, so I can make sure we're all safe," I state.

Sheena understands what I'm saying and informs me that she'll do her best to remember pertinent details as they arise. I'm very upset that she neglected to tell me about this Marcus fellow because he very well could be working with the others to harm Sheena. Damn, the plot thickens one more time. I wonder if I should have Sheena call the detective to tell him about the threats that Marcus made. There are pros and cons to telling the detective about him. In my opinion, the cons outweigh the pros, so I decide against Sheena informing Detective Mosely.

We swing by Rachel's house and pick the boys up and go back home. It's been another long day to say the least. I'm extremely reluctant to let Sheena out of my sight for even a moment. I know Devon's doing his best, but nothing seems to happen to Sheena when I'm with her, so maybe it's best if I stick to her like glue. I know my boys don't need to be around any of this. I think they may need some more time with their grandmother in New Jersey. I'll make the call to my mom as soon as I get home to see if she's willing to watch them for a little while. Sheena may not like that too much, but she'll have to acquiesce this time. I'm not wavering on this one bit. We arrive at the house and go inside. I chat with Sheena before I call my mom.

"There has been too much violence going on around here lately and I don't want the boys around any of it, so I'm gonna see if my mom is willing to keep them for a while until this gets sorted out," I say.

"Sage, I don't know about that. That's an indefinite amount of time and I don't like the idea of them being away for who knows how long. Those are our kids and we can't just ship them off like a FedEx package," Sheena expresses.

"I'm sorry you feel that way. You told me the other day that's it's my job to protect this family and I'll do just that. If that means letting the boys spend time with their grandmother, then that's what it's going to be. I can't allow anything to happen to them. If my mom agrees to keep the boys, that's the route we're going," I explain.

"I don't like it, but you're the leader of the family and if you say it's a go, I support your decision," Sheena replies.

Sheena and I talk a little longer about all that's going on and how she feels. Next, I call my mom to see what she thinks about keeping the boys. She's excited about being able to watch her grandchildren and agrees to have them. Another plus is that Sheena's mom will also be able to see Devin and Deric while they're in Linden. My mom agrees to meet me in Delaware, so I don't have to drive all the way to Linden and back. I decide the best thing to do is leave out immediately. We pack the boys and their belongings up and get on the road.

We make it to Delaware and back in a few hours with no incident. I know Sheena and I will miss our sons, but we both decide that it'll be better to miss them for a week or two than to miss them for a lifetime. It's just better to err on the side of caution. Sheena goes to hit the shower and then goes to sleep. I have too much on my mind than to go to sleep. Instead, I stay up and keep my eye on my cameras.

The next morning, I'm awakened by Sheena. Apparently, I fell asleep at my desk in my office. I didn't even know I fell asleep. I guess I was sleepier than I thought. Sheena laughs at me for falling asleep in here. I regret falling asleep in my office chair too because now I have a terrible cramp in my neck. I alert Sheena to the presence of the cramp and she kindly begins to massage my neck for me. Her hands are heavenly! It's almost like they contain a healing elixir. My eyes are closed and I'm almost asleep when Sheena screams out.

"Oh my goodness Sage! Look!" Sheena screams.

My eyes instantaneously pop open to see what Sheena wants me to see. She points to the security monitor. The screen shows Dion walking in front of the house peering again. Oh, hell no! Enough is enough. I can't believe he's back again. I've been nice for far too long. I knew I should have taken him out the other night. Well, he's on my property now and he's all mine. I look at all of the camera angles I have and it appears that he's alone. I was really hoping to see him with the other guys, but I guess I couldn't be so lucky. I'll make my move on him now.

"Sheena, you know what to do? Are you ready?" I ask.

"Yes, I told you that when the time came I'd be ready. Now is the time and I'm ready. Let's do this," Sheena orates.

Sheena heads to the garage and jumps in the car. She lifts the garage door and backs out of the garage. As she backs out of the driveway, Dion beelines for her car with something in his hand. He yells her name and seems to have a bone to pick with her. When he gets about three feet from the car, Sheena hits the brakes and ducks down. I'm slumped over in the front seat and pop up as soon as she ducks down and shoot Dion two times in the chest. I spring from out of the car and run over to him.

I open the palm of his hand and take out what he's holding. Sheena jumps out the car and joins me. Dion is gasping for air as he chokes on his blood. She dials 911 and they say someone is on the way. I'm confused as to why he's carrying what he's carrying. It's a picture of Devin and Deric when they were newly born. I pass the picture to Sheena and she's also surprised. She reads a small note on the back of the photo that's in Eric's handwriting. He wrote a short note as if it were from the boys.

"To the best godfather in the world. Love Deric and Devin," Sheena reads.

Obviously, he was named as the boys' godfather when they were both believed to be Eric's sons. That's a tough break, but why is he here to begin with? He doesn't have permission to be here at my home lurking about.

Sheena asks in a panic, "What are you doing here Dion?"

"I wanted to see the kids. Eric told me about the situation with the boys, but I never stopped loving them. Sheena, you never brought them back around. I just wanted to see how they were doing," Dion states in an extremely tender voice right before he dies.

Sheena is broken because she realizes that I've just killed an innocent man who was only coming to see his former godchild. However, I don't feel badly because we had no way of knowing what he was doing. With all the recent activity at the house, we had no way of knowing what he was planning to do. The cops and ambulance are on the way. There's no need for the ambulance to rush because Dion's long gone.

What a terrible way to start off the day. Sheena won't be making it to the office today for sure. Officer Mosely shows up again at the house to take a statement. We don't tell him that we saw Dion on the security camera before we exited the house to set him up. We only tell him that we were backing out of the driveway and he ran up to the car yelling and that we feared for our lives with all of the recent happenings and I shot him.

"I understand. Like I said before Ms. Mills, you are one lucky person because all of these attempts don't normally go in one's favor. You really pissed off somebody pretty good for them to keep coming for you," speaks Detective Mosely.

"I guess I've made some enemies along the way, but it wasn't from anything I did. The enemies come from me just being who I am. I don't apologize for being who I am. Officer, I know this man. He's the cousin of my ex-boyfriend, Eric Burns," I respond.

"Really, he must be upset about the way things

went with his cousin and was gonna retaliate against you," Detective Mosely says.

"I really don't know what he was going to do, sir. He rushed the car yelling something and before you know it, he was on the ground shot. He seemed perturbed about something, but we never got to find out," I explain.

Officer Mosely has no choice but to take our story. The man was on my property and was the cousin of a guy who tried to kill Sheena. Additionally, we're the only ones here to tell the story. Officer Mosely does find it strange that Dion doesn't have a weapon to cause Sheena harm with, but doesn't make an issue of it. I take the detective inside to show him the security footage of what happened. He watches it and it matches the story we told him. As part of the investigation, Detective Mosely takes a copy of the video with him. Hours later, the coroner, detective, and the cops leave my house. Sheena and I process what happened and then I take her to her office to handle an unexpected situation that couldn't wait to be handled.

Sheena didn't intend to go to the office today, but when there's a lot of work to be done and pressing issues, you have to handle your business. I need to stop by the lounge, but it's nothing pressing. I do have to be there tomorrow for sure. All of the new appliances are being delivered and installed tomorrow. The following day, all of the furniture is being delivered, so it's going to be a busy few days for the lounge. I plan to have the lounge reopened in the next two weeks. I make a few calls while Sheena's in and out of meetings.

CHAPTER 15
Sheena's Attacker's Perspective

I am beyond angry and frustrated. I've tried to kill Sheena several times and it just isn't working. I can't give up. All I have to do is be successful one time. I've been so close that I could taste her dying. I have to try harder or try a new approach. When I get my payback for what has been done, it's going to be sweeter than project Kool-Aid. I'm pissed that I no longer have a gun because I dropped it in the bathroom at the hotel. Now, I can't just walk up to her and blow her fucking brains out! I hate knowing that she's still breathing.

Sheena Mills doesn't deserve to take another breath. She shouldn't be spending time with her family and friends any longer. I'm going to settle the score and make things right. What can I do to get close enough to snatch her life from her?

Maybe I can pretend to be a new client for her and get her that way. Yeah, that's definitely a viable option, but it's highly unlikely that she'll come to meet me somewhere with all that's going on. She knows what I look like and will scream at the top of her lungs as soon as she sees me.

That means that someone is going to have to draw her out for me or I'll have to follow her and get her that way. Hmm, Devon is her bodyguard. Maybe I'll get at him and have him pull her out for me. If I'm lucky, she'll be crossing the street or be in a parking lot and I'll be able to run her over like an opossum in the streets. I'm sure her friends don't have bodyguards. I could grab one of them and have them call her over and then I can get my revenge. I have so many options that I don't know which one I'll use. Sheena's time on earth is running very, very short.

I may need to lay low for a little while and let everyone's defenses subside before I plan my next attack on Sheena. The police presence around her will probably be very high anyway. I thought making a quick move on her at the house would be my best chance of getting her, but I fell short. Hmm, she has a wedding coming up and that may afford me the best chance of killing her.

CHAPTER 16
Sage's Perspective

It's been quite some time since I killed Dion at my house. The investigation the police conducted didn't last very long. It was pretty much an open and shut case. I'm happy it went that way because I really don't have time to be caught up in time consuming tasks that aren't productive. The last couple of months have been pretty quiet on the home front. I still can't sleep comfortably because Sheena's attacker is still at large. I really don't like the fact that we have what I think is a pretty clear image of the guy, but the police still haven't gotten any leads on him. I've even put the picture into the hands of some of my contacts and they haven't gotten any leads for me either. It's almost like he doesn't exist.

I haven't let my attempts to track down Sheena's attacker deter me from my goal of opening the lounge. It took longer than I originally thought it would due to delays from new building codes. The good thing is that it's all behind me because the lounge is finally having its grand reopening tonight.

We are really rolling out all the bells and whistles tonight. Everybody's getting in for free tonight and we even have free food and champagne until it runs out. I've also arranged for a few celebrities to perform for the guests later in the evening.

Social media is buzzing with the news of the grand reopening. The trending topic in D.C. is In the Mix. I'm sure the news of the reopening will cause people to flock here all night. The fire wasn't all bad now that I look back on it. I've increased the maximum capacity of the lounge and added more booths and tables. That means profits are going to go up! I'll be able to recoup the money I've lost from the lounge being closed in no time.

The place is packed like old times. The way it looks in here right now would make someone think that the lounge never closed. The energy in here is so palpable that you can scoop it up and bag it. It feels good to be back in business. It's been a long time coming. It seems like so much has changed since In the Mix was open. My lounge will eventually resume its place as the number one nightlife spot in D.C.

Sheena is here tonight with her crew. They're sitting in their favorite booth and celebrating like they've done so many times before. Sheena and her girls still have plenty of dudes flocking to their table. Unfortunately for the guys, they're all getting turned down left and right. I'm not the jealous type, so I find it comical, but I'm different from a lot of guys. Ilesha's and Rachel's boyfriends are in here tonight and neither one of them is as understanding as I am about all the guys who are incessantly approaching them.

I know where I stand with Sheena, so there's

nothing for me to worry about. I'm working the crowd and thanking people for coming out. I see a lot of the same faces coming through the lounge's doors who patronized the club before we closed. I appreciate their continued support and that's the reason why I'm giving away so much for free tonight. In order to be a good businessman, I feel you have to give back to the people who help make you successful. It's only right. No relationship should be one sided.

The music and food are great. As much as I want to relax, I really can't. I still need to keep my head on a swivel because I don't know who may try to get in here. Monster is running the door with another member of my security team. There's no way Sheena's attacker will get past Monster and besides that, there's a crowd in here and he'd be certain to get caught. Even if he got somebody else to try to get at Sheena, it wouldn't make sense.

I continue making my rounds and checking on the kitchen staff. I walk to the bar and notice that the bar could use a couple more bottles of alcohol. I shoot to the closet to retrieve the bottles and head back to the bar. While I'm restocking the bar, I glance over in Sheena's direction. She has an unpleasant look on her face and she summons me over to her. I urgently walk over to see what's going on.

"Honey, what's up with the unpleasant facial expression?" I inquire.

"It's probably nothing, but I just wanted you to know that I saw Marcus. He came over to the table, but didn't say anything. He just cut me and my girls a funny look and kept on going," Sheena voices.

"Is that right? The same one who threatened you

the day you were kidnapped? If so, where is he?" I ask.

Sheena walks around with me for a few minutes, but we don't spot him. I'm perturbed at the fact that we can't find him because I'd love to have a conversation with him. The reality is that depending on what he says during that conversation, it may be more than just a conversation. Sheena and I walk back to her table and have a short discussion. I instruct one of my security personnel to keep a close eye on Sheena and her friends. I walk to the front of the lounge to talk to Monster.

"Everything alright out here?" I ask.

Monster answers, "Everything's smooth out here. I had to turn a couple people away for not being dressed properly, but other than that, it's all good."

I question, "Are you keeping a count of the number of people we have inside? You know we can't have any issues with the fire marshal?"

"I have the counter right here. We're still a little under the maximum capacity. You know I got this under control. This isn't my first rodeo," Monster replies.

"I know you have it covered. It's opening night, so I'm just a little over cautious. It's not that I don't think you're on point," I voice.

Monster states, "Cool, because I have your back, but you already know that. I'll make sure all of the outside stuff is taken care of."

"Alright, one last thing, do you have a list of the names of everyone who came through the doors tonight?" I ask.

"Yeah, Omar has the list right there," Devon responds.

Omar hands me the list and I take the names of the people who have already signed in. I give Omar the clipboard back, so he can continue capturing the names of the people going forward. I take the list to my office and look it over. I'm perusing the list to see if I can find Marcus's name on it. I'm looking through the first several pages of the list and don't see his name. I guess I'll have to look through the entire list because there's no telling when Marcus entered the club.

Finally, I run into a name of Marcus Mullins on the list. However, I don't stop there because there may be more than one Marcus on the list. I continue exploring the tabulation of attendees of the club tonight and eventually get finished. I was only able to find one Marcus on the list, so I'll run with it. I walk back into the lounge and strut to the DJ booth. I tell the DJ to turn the music down after the song finishes, but not to turn it off completely. I want to keep the music playing to maintain the patron's attention, but I also want it to be low enough for me to be able to talk over it. The song ends, so the DJ lowers the volume on the next song as I asked.

"Everybody let me have your attention. I don't want to kill your night with a bunch of talking, but I did want to take a moment to thank you all for coming out. It means a lot and I couldn't be more moved by you ladies and gentlemen joining In the Mix for its grand reopening," I vocalize.

I continue delivering a short impromptu speech to the crowd. They clap in approval to what I'm saying. They're showing a lot of love tonight. When you spread love, you get love back. I tell the people in the crowd that it's time to give out a door prize. Many people are surprised because they weren't given any tickets or anything else that would make them think door prizes were being given out.

I call out the first name that's on the list. Fortunately, she's still in the lounge when I call her name and comes running to the DJ booth where I'm standing. I hand her a crisp fifty-dollar bill, give her a hug, and thank her for coming out tonight. She takes a picture of us for Snapchat and runs off pumping her hands in the air. I call another name off the list and repeat the same course of action as I did with the person before. She also takes a picture with me and posts it to social media. I call Marcus as the last winner of the fifty-dollar door prize. I don't know if he's still here, but I have to find out. Calling him as a winner is the only way I can think of to find out what he looks like.

There's a long moment of silence in the lounge while we wait for Marcus to make himself known. I wait as long as I can, but Marcus isn't coming to the DJ booth, so I go to call another name on the list to make it look like these door prizes are for real. If I don't put another name in the place of Marcus's, someone may become suspicious. To my delight, just before I call another name, a man's voice screams out from the direction of the restroom. He claims to be Marcus. Marcus was in the restroom when I initially called his name. I shake his hand and give him the fifty dollars for being a winner. Marcus, being the flashy and cocky guy he is, pulls out a wad of cash and puts the fifty in with it. Every patron in the club saw his pocket full of money.

We also take a picture together. My little charade worked out perfectly. It cost me one hundred and fifty dollars to find out who Marcus is, but it was well worth it. I don't think anyone even caught onto what I was up to. My stunt will have all the customers talking about how nice I am and I'll benefit from the kind words for sure. I benefit personally from this too. Since I know what Marcus looks like now, I'll be able to keep a tab on him to see if he's working with the guy who has been trying to hurt Sheena.

The rest of the night flows seamlessly. There are no fights, everyone's in good spirits, and the bar is staying packed. I have my eye on Marcus. I checked my security camera of the parking lot and was able to see what kind of car he drove here. He's riding clean in his big body Benz. That's going to help me out, but be the reason for his demise. I have to follow him out of here tonight to hopefully see where he lives. If I don't find out tonight, I may not get the chance again.

I leave my office and stroll back into the restaurant and bar area with all of the customers. I see Marcus dancing around and I want to go snatch him up to interrogate him, but I know that would be pointless. Instead, I go over to Sheena and tell her that I'm leaving for the night. She's surprised that I'm leaving on such a big night before all of the customers depart. She knows that I must have something important to do if I'm about to leave.

"You serious? Are you feeling okay?" Sheena asks in a tone of disbelief.

"Yeah, I'm serious. I have to check something out, so I'm going to roll. I'll let Monster know that he'll be taking you home tonight," I answer.

"No, I'll just leave with you," Sheena replies.

"No, the hell you won't. I told you that I'm going

to check something out and that's it! Damn it, I need you to just listen for once!" I say assertively.

Several people see Sheena and me have a slight argument before I bounce from the club. I'm sure many people will speculate as to why we argued, but the truth is that it's none of their business. I've never been one to share my business with other people or answer questions about why I do what I do. I head out the door of the lounge, jump in my car, and bounce.

CHAPTER 17
Sheena's Perspective

I head to the bar to go get another drink. I'm tired of sitting at this table. On the way to the bar, I see Marcus and he's giving me the bedroom eyes. I can't even front like he isn't looking good. I shoot him a slightly inviting look back as I lean on the bar with my booty accentuated. To my delight, he starts making his way over to me. The bartenders are busy fixing drinks, so I wait my turn. Marcus makes his way over to me.

"I thought I saw you smile at me when I looked over your way. I wasn't sure, so I figured I'd come investigate," Marcus utters.

I reply coyly, "Maybe I did, but then again maybe I didn't. You'll just have to determine that for yourself."

"Well, since you are leaving it up to me, I determine that you did smile at me. I also think that you should let me buy you a drink. Anything you want you can have," Marcus voices confidently.

"Marcus, this is my fiancé's lounge. Everything I

order in here is free, so if you're trying to impress me with a drink, you have to come harder than that," I drop on Marcus.

Marcus responds humorously, "That's right. I can't argue that and since that's the case you should order me some wings and a Long Island. I'm just saying, since you're royalty in here. And that was an interesting choice of words."

"Boy, please. What have you done to earn my hookup? You do know my royalty label extends far outside the confines of these walls? And what was so interesting about my words?" I ask.

"I can't even lie. I've done nothing to get your hookup. I've heard several times that your walls are royal. The way you said, 'cum harder' was interesting to me," Marcus answers.

"Damn right you haven't. In fact, you really don't deserve my conversation right now. Last time we spoke, you were tripping. I bet you would like to know about my walls. As far as my words of 'come harder', they were purely innocent," I reply. "You so damn nasty!"

"Yeah, I was tripping, but for some reason you're still here chatting with me. I would like to find out how royal your walls are since you mention it. I really don't think you or your comments are so innocent to be honest," Marcus remarks.

"Maybe I'm talking to you because my man is tripping. Maybe, I want to get you a drink. And maybe I'm not so innocent. And without question, my walls are royal," I comment.

"Yeah, I saw that argument. I looked over in your direction and saw him raising his hand at you, but that's none of my business, so I'll take that Long

Island now," Marcus says.

"Yes, he's certainly tripping tonight. I don't know what that was about," I verbalize.

"You know how men do sometimes. We act out when we're stressed or we don't get our way," Marcus explains.

"Let me get a Long Island and a shot of Patron," I say as I turn to the bartender.

The bartender gives me the drinks and I hand the Long Island to Marcus. The bartender looks at me funny when she sees me hand him the drink. She works for Sage, so I know she's wondering what's going on. I decide to walk Marcus away from the bar, so we can talk some more.

Marcus states, "Wait, you forgot about my wings."

"I didn't forget about your wings. We don't have enough time for the wings," I utter.

"Well, what time does the kitchen close?" Marcus asks. "Didn't you say you're royalty here?"

"Hell yeah, I'm royalty, but I'm not worried about the kitchen closing. I just don't have all night to be in here. I do have to go home and you did say you want to see how royal my walls are," I verbalize.

"Oh, yeah, that's what I said. It's probably best if we leave now then. No, need to beat around the bush in here," Marcus suggests.

Marcus guzzles his Long Island and I sit my drink down. I tell him that he has to walk out before me because Devon is at the front door and there's no way that he'll let me leave with anybody. He walks out and I go to Ilesha and tell her to start making a big scene over something. I know Devon will come to check on the situation himself and I'll be able to slide out the front door. Ilesha starts cursing a guy out who really didn't do anything to her and as expected Devon comes to investigate. I scoot out the front door, go down the block, and jump in Marcus's car.

"I love your car. Hell, I can see myself driving this," I say.

"Thanks, this is my baby. I just bought it like a month ago. It only had three miles on it when I got it," Marcus boasts.

"So, is it a 2017 or 2018?" I ask.

"Baby, this is a 2018. I didn't want the 2017 cause it's too close to 2018," Marcus responds.

"I know that's right! Well, we have to go to your place tonight cause I live with Sage," I inform.

"Shit, my kids are at my house with the babysitter, so we can't go there. It's cool though, I have a hookup at the Ritz-Carlton, so we can just go there," Marcus tells.

"Right, we definitely can't go to your place. Umm, no! Even though this is gonna be a one-time thing, I can't risk being seen at a hotel. Sage knows damn near all of D.C.," I explain.

"I feel you on that, but you're gonna want more than one time after I put this on you. Only other thing I can offer is for us to park somewhere," Marcus indicates.

"Hmm, the car would be easy, but I don't feel like being cramped up in the car. Besides, I wanna fuck you good and let you feel all this good pussy I got. Listen, I have a key to my girl's house, so we can just go there. She's still at In the Mix and I know she's closing it out," I report.

We drive over to what I say is Ilesha's house and park the car. As soon as we park the car, Marcus opens his door to get out and I do too. Unfortunately, as soon as his feet hit the ground, he is met by Sage who swiftly shoots him several times with an unregistered gun. I run down the street and jump in Sage's car. Marcus falls against his car and slides lifelessly to the ground. Sage runs over to Marcus' body and snatches off the white gold chain that Marcus has around his neck and reaches in his pocket to remove the wad of cash he flashed in the club earlier. Sage walks down the street, jumps in his car, and we pull off. Sage drops me off down the street from the lounge. I retrieve my phone that I stashed down the street from the lounge in order to make it look like I never left the area. Sage took his phone home when he left the lounge and set it to answer automatically after one ring.

I called him before I stashed the phone to create an alibi if we ever need one. The story will be that we had an argument, so Sage stormed out of the lounge. Then, I called him in an effort to settle the argument that we previously had. On the drive home, Sage throws the chain he ripped from Marcus's neck and the gun he used to shoot him with in the Howard University Reservoir.

When Sage arrives home, he takes off the clothes and throws them in the fireplace and burns them until they're all ashes. We had to make it look like a robbery that turned into a homicide. Marcus made a big mistake when he flashed all of that money at the club and we decided to use that against him. Sage didn't want to take any chances with Marcus being part of the plot against me. He felt like it was best for us to make a move tonight, so we faked that argument to put it underway.

CHAPTER 18
Sheena's Perspective

I don't think I've ever posted so many pictures and messages to social media in my life. It's almost my wedding day and I'm feeling good, so I'm snapping pictures galore. Not to mention, this hotel is the bomb, so why not show it off? My girls and I have been on one big happy rollercoaster all day. We've been taking pictures in the room, in the elevator, in front of the hotel and even in the bathroom. It's been crazy!

I can't believe that in less than twenty-four hours, I'll no longer be a girlfriend or fiancée because I'll be a wife! It seems like I'm living a dream right now. One of the reasons I'm so happy about it and in disbelief is because the road I traveled to get here was filled with many bumps – no, mountains. I've had children, been engaged to someone else, had two boyfriends simultaneously, and even almost died. Life is very unpredictable. Life is so uncertain from moment to moment and I truly didn't know if I'd make it to this point.

I'm almost at the altar. I want it so badly that I can taste it, but I wouldn't fast forward to tomorrow though. My mom always tells me to savor the moment and don't rush things. This moment is awesome. To know that someone wants to be with me forever as much as I want to be with him drives me wild inside. I'm blessed to be marrying the man of my dreams and realities. Unfortunately, everyone is not as fortunate as I am.

I'll remember this moment with my girls forever. Not that I'll ever forget the other memories we've shared and there have been some great ones, but tonight will be at the top of the list. Tonight is my last night with them as a single woman and my last night to be free as a bird. It's almost like tonight is the ending of a special time in my life and tomorrow marks a new era of my life. I'll always cherish the time with my sisters. They've made my life much more enjoyable and meaningful.

Tonight is going to be crazy and wild to say the least. Me, my sisters, and several other girls are in Ilesha's hotel room waiting for the male and female strippers to arrive. The entire idea of my bachelorette party was all Ilesha's. I told her that I didn't care to have one, but she wouldn't hear of not having one, so I agreed to let her do her thing. I know it's my marriage, but Ilesha and Rachel are taking as much jubilation in this as I am. If she wants to send me off right, I won't stop her. I won't partake in too much scandalous behavior because there are too many females who are not in our circle and may have loose lips. I definitely don't need anyone telling my business to the world. Not to mention, everyone in here has their cell phones in their hand. I refuse to be the bride who's on Facebook, Snapchat, Instagram, and Twitter looking like a fool. If I go viral, it'll be for something that's proper and of a high standard.

There's a knock at the door that startles me because it's so loud and hard. I think that it's the police until everyone starts clapping their hands because they know it's the strippers. Ilesha opens the door and four men along with three women enter the room. Rachel turns the music up as soon as they enter. They are all dressed in black attire. The men have on black boots, cargo pants, black officer's coats, and skullies. These men are very militant and handsome. The women are dressed in all black heels, tight black skirts, with halter tops, and their hair pulled back in ponytails. They are ultra-sexy!

"Who is the bride-to-be?" one of the male strippers asks.

All of the women point to me at the same time. I'm raising my hand and smiling extremely big. Two of the strippers rush over to me and lift me in the air. They whisk me to the center of the penthouse suite Ilesha has us in. They seat me in a chair that one of the female dancers has setup for me. Tonight is all about me I see. I'm actually glad that female entertainers are here. However, it's not that I want to see them dance for sexual gratification. It's more so for research and informative reasons. If I see one of these women do a trick that I really like, I'll take note of it and use it tomorrow after the wedding on Sage. Hell, I'll really blow his mind with some new moves.

I'm sitting center stage and the music is blasting. Rachel put together a playlist of all of the songs we used to party to growing up. She's so thoughtful. Rachel knows that the music will trigger a lot of old and great memories for me and really aid in me enjoying the night. I'm sitting in the chair bopping my head to the music while two of the dancers start dancing in front of me while removing their shirts. I want to get up and start dancing too, but I refrain. I would get up, but I don't want them to think I'm getting up to dance with them. I'd only be getting up because this is my song! I'm just chillaxing though.

One guy's shirt is off and his ab muscles look like they are chiseled out of a stone because they are so perfect. His chest and stomach are so oiled up that his skin is like one big reflector. Ilesha hands me several dollar bills to tip him with. Hey, it's not my money, so I tip him. He's working hard for the money, but I don't touch him though. Instead, I just throw the singles in the air and make it rain on him. I don't want the other guy to feel left out, so I make it rain on him too. Ilesha and Rachel are tipping the other entertainers and so are the other women in the room.

The strippers tease the ladies in the room by taking their time dropping their pants. Let's be real, all of the ladies love nice chests and stomachs, but they really want to see some big dicks. I want to see a big dick too, but it's not in this room right now. It's somewhere in Sage's pants and I can't wait to get to it! The female dancers are twerking on some of the women in here and I'm taking notes. I'm watching the moves they're doing and deciding which ones I'll do and which ones I know I can't do. I'm not trying to hurt myself on my wedding night. Oh my goodness, did she just fall into a full split? Well, that's out of the question because I can't do that.

The night is going the way I always saw my

bachelorette party going. I have my girls, good music, alcohol even though I'm not drinking tonight, and a million laughs. Some of the women in here decide to go way further than I ever would have. One girl is giving a stripper head on the couch. I never saw that happening and a female dancer is eating one of my old college friend's pussy. Where they do that at?

As much as I'm enjoying myself, I think it's time for me to pardon myself. I really didn't want the party to begin with, but I appeased my girl, but now it's time for me to go have some chill time. I refuse to look less than my best on my wedding day. My room is down the hall from the suite that the party is in, so I walk down to it. I'm not ready to go to sleep, so I get on social media and post about tonight and how I must be getting old because I'm in my room alone hiding from my own party. Several people reply to my posts. Some of the women who reply are married or are mothers and totally understand my wanting to chill. Ilesha and Rachel told me that they'll come to check on me later. I'm cool with that and I hope I'm not messing up their fun.

CHAPTER 19
Sheena's Attacker's Perspective

It seems like all of Washington D.C. is going to be at that wedding tomorrow. I guess Sage thinks he's the shit, since he's having a big wedding. He really isn't all that in my book. It really doesn't matter who's at that wedding tomorrow because there's not going to be one. Those guests are going to be madder than hell when the bride doesn't arrive. She's not going to miss the wedding because she's having cold feet, but she's going to miss it because she's going to be dead!

I have what I need to get this done and it's going down tonight. I have to end this tonight because the police have my photograph and it's been circulating. I've been able to stay under the radar for a while, but I know my days are numbered, so I have to make my move. Where's my phone at? It's time for me to get out of here and head to that hotel. On the way to the hotel where Sheena is staying, I stop by the store and grab a dozen roses and a box of chocolate.

I pull into the parking garage and stand outside of my car for a moment. I don't go inside because I need a little help with my plan. Moments later, a guy pulls up and gets out of his car and starts walking toward the hotel lobby. I stop him and chat with him for a minute.

"What's up man?" I ask.

"Not much on my end. Bout to holla at my girl. It's gonna be a good night," he replies as he chuckles. "Looks like you're gonna have a good night too with those flowers and candy."

I state, "Most definitely. At least that's the plan. Really, I could use your help. I'll even pay you fifty bucks for your trouble."

"Man, I don't know. Just depends on what you want me to do," the guy responds.

"Bro, it's nothing. I just want to surprise my girl with these flowers and candy. I'm just getting back in town from being overseas and she doesn't know it. She's here at her homegirl's bachelorette party, so I wanna drop these flowers off, so she can show off in front of her friends. Make her feel real good and really surprise her," I explain.

"That's a good idea man. She's gonna melt in your arms when she sees you!" he utters.

"Yeah, I'm gonna have her in my arms for sure," I say without him knowing the true meaning of what I mean.

"I'll help out. What do you need me to do?" he inquires.

I speak, "Bro, it's simple. You'll just knock on the door and when she asks who it is, you'll just tell her it's a delivery from Sage. She'll look through the peep hole, see you and then open the door. After that, I'll pop up with the big surprise."

The guy agrees to the plan and we walk into the

hotel. We can't get to the penthouse suite floor from the elevator because you have to have a special key and of course I don't have one. It's no big issue though because we just get off on the highest floor the elevator takes us and walk up three more flights of steps to their floor. Me and the guy make small talk on the way to Sheena's room. We make it to her room P312 and the guy helping me knocks on the door.

"Who is it?" Sheena asks from inside the room.

"Delivery for Miss Mills," he replies.

"I didn't order anything," Sheena says.

I can tell that she's standing right in front of the door because of the sound of her voice. She's most likely looking through the peep hole to inspect things. The dude helping me tells her that it's a surprise delivery from Sage McMillian as we rehearsed. Thankfully, Sheena takes the bait and opens the door to receive her flowers. If only she knew that these flowers would be her death flowers, she wouldn't be opening the door. As the door opens, I hit the guy over the head and he falls to the floor knocked out. I didn't want to hurt him, but I couldn't risk him wanting to be a hero and attempt to help Sheena if he heard a scuffle somehow. I would have had to kill him at that point, so really this guy should thank me for only busting him upside the head.

I push through the door and I'm ready to attack, but to my confusion I'm hit over the head with a very hard object and am immediately dazed. How did Sheena know I was coming? I fall down to one knee and take an eight count. I clear my head and then I see Sage standing in the room. What the hell is he doing here? Isn't he supposed to be at his bachelor party? He looks in his phone and begins talking. I hear Sheena talking on the phone and it becomes apparent that Sage is FaceTiming her. She was never in the room at all. Sage turns the phone toward my face and asks Sheena if I'm the guy who kidnapped her. Sheena informs him that I am the guy.

"Okay honey. Let me end this thing. I'll call you in a few minutes when the cops leave," Sage says to Sheena.

"No, I want to stay on the phone. Don't hang up. I want to hear and see what's going on. I deserve to see this," Sheena words.

Sage agrees to Sheena's request and props his phone up to allow Sheena to see what's going on. They must be crazy if they think that I'm going to sit still while the cops come to arrest me. Sage made a bad mistake by not continuing to pummel me with whatever he hit me with. He's allowing me to regain my composure after that initial blow. He'll pay the price for that right now.

"Sage, I hope you don't think that I'm gonna sit in this room and wait for the cops to come because I'm not," I verbalize. "You'll be dead first."

Sheena yells, "Sage, just kill him. He doesn't deserve to live anyway!"

"I got this honey… I'll handle it. Just chill," Sage states.

"You had your shot and now I'm gonna whoop your ass. Sheena, you're gonna watch your man die. I wish it were you here instead of Sage, so he can live with the pain I do," I word angrily.

"Why do you think I'm gonna die today? Also, what's your beef with Sheena anyway? Why do you want her dead so badly?" Sage asks. "What has she done to you?"

"You're gonna die today because I'm going to kill you and my beef isn't with her, it's with you for what you did. I want her to die, so you can suffer," I respond.

"Man, that's bullshit! I've never met you a day in my life. There's no way you have a problem with me," Sage verbalizes.

"You're right, we've never met, but you have met my godmother Mrs. Kline. She spent her last days depressed and died with a broken heart because of you. That's why I want Sheena dead because I want you to experience the same heartbreak she did," I explain.

"Sage, what's going on over there? What exactly is he talking? Did he say that this is all your fault stemming from something you did?" Sheena asks wildly.

Sage looks down at the phone and tells Sheena that it's a long story and he'll explain it to her later. He's distracted and I have to make a move now to take him down and get out of here. I pull the knife out of my pocket that I was going to use to kill Sheena with. Sheena tells Sage that she wants to know what I said, but he won't tell her. Sage's attention is on the phone and not on me, so I rise up from my knee and lunge toward him. My calculations about him not being focused on me are off by a mile because Sage whips out his gun and shoots me several times and I fall to the floor.

CHAPTER 20
Sheena's Perspective

"Sage, what happened? Are you there?" I ask frantically.

"Baby, I'm here and he's dead. Let me hang up, so I can call the authorities. In fact, you should come down here," Sage words.

"K. I'm on my way," I say.

Sage is on the phone with the cops when I get to the room. The guy is on the floor dead. I've seen too many dead bodies in my short lifespan. I'm glad it's not me or one of my loved ones. Sage orchestrated his magic again. All of that posting my whereabouts to social media paid off because this guy took the bait. Earlier in the day, I took a picture of a hotel room door, but it wasn't my room. It was really the room Sage was in hoping the guy would take the bait and he did.

Sage didn't want to take the chance of me actually being in the room if the dude showed up. Officer Mosely arrives with several cops and they take our statements. I tell them that I wasn't in the room and don't have a clue as to what happened. My story is that I showed up after the guy was dead. Sage handles all of the talking to the cops.

"So, the guy just showed up at your door?" asks one of the officers.

"Pretty much and just pushed his way in after knocking out the delivery boy. A short fight ensued and I shot him," Sage reports. "I'm sure the hotel has video surveillance. I'm sure you'll find the delivery boy somewhere."

"My guy is in the security room watching it now. He'll radio me in a minute. Well, Miss Mills like I've said plenty of times that you're very lucky to be alive. I'm glad you aren't the victim," Detective Mosely says.

"I guess I really do have nine lives Detective. I may have used them all up after this long ordeal. I hope not though," I reply.

"Let's hope not. Sage, I tried contacting you earlier, but I didn't get you. I left a message for you to call me," Detective Mosely says.

"Sorry, I missed it. I didn't know you called. I was probably busy finalizing some wedding stuff. The big day is tomorrow!" Sage tells.

"I was calling to tell you that my guy in ballistics ran the bullets from the ceiling in the bathroom in the hotel and they matched the ballistics from the bullet that was pulled out of you the day you were shot," Detective Mosely informs. "Also, the prints from the bathroom we got off the gun he had matched the prints from Sheena's house. It appears that this guy really had it out for the both of you."

I say, "Oh my goodness! He was really trying to kill us and we don't even know him. I mean, I've never seen him in my life until all of this started."

"So, this is the fucker who tried to kill me?" Sage asks the Detective.

"Yes, it seems to be that way. We don't know what his motive was if you don't know him, but whatever it was, he was willing to die for it," speaks the Detective.

They take Sage's gun for evidence as they always do. They have to file their reports and close the case. The cops leave and I go back to my room to get some sleep. I have a wedding tomorrow and I'm not missing it for the world. Sage goes home to spend the night. I fall asleep comfortably in my hotel room bed.

I wake up to my girls knocking on my room door. I jump out of bed and let them in. We have a full day of prepping for the wedding. We have to get our makeup, hair, and nails done today. My girls are being super helpful and are ensuring that I don't have to stress over anything. Ilesha is staying on top of the wedding planner, so I don't have to. The hours before the wedding fly by. I'm sitting in the bridal suite when Rachel and Ilesha walk in with the bridal party.

"Sheena, it's time. You look beautiful, my sister," says Rachel.

"Girl, it's your damn day, so if you're not ready to go out there, don't. Rachel is right. You look gorgeous in your dress. I'm glad you're getting married because you've been nasty as hell over the last two years," Ilesha states. "Bitch, I hope you've been heavy on the Kegel exercises."

"Girl, you belong in an insane asylum because you're crazy as hell. My goods are nice, tight, and fresh," I assert.

I've waited for this day my entire life and I'm marrying the man of my dreams. Sage has been the love of my life, since we met at In the Mix a long time ago. The journey has been a long one to say the least, but I've made it to my destination and I'm happy. I walk to the doors and in what seems to be slow motion, then they open. I walk through the doors to everybody standing and looking in my direction. My groom stands upfront waiting to claim me. My emotions are overwhelming and a tear trickles down my cheek. My long-awaited wedding day is **finally** here.

LOVE THIS BOOK AND WANT MORE?

VISIT RYANHODGEBOOKS.COM

MORE BOOKS BY RYAN

The Deception Series:
*Web of Deception**
*Wrath of Deception**
*Will of Deception**
*Rape by Deception***

Historical Science Fiction:
Reversed World Power

*Adult romance
**Suspense Thriller. Spin-off of other novels in series

www.ingramcontent.com/pod-product-compliance
Lightning Source LLC
Chambersburg PA
CBHW070120260626

47160CB00004B/1559